Julius Chambers, Julius Chambers, Julius Chambers

Missing

A Romance

Julius Chambers, Julius Chambers, Julius Chambers

Missing
A Romance

ISBN/EAN: 9783743467941

Manufactured in Europe, USA, Canada, Australia, Japa

Cover: Foto ©Andreas Hilbeck / pixelio.de

Manufactured and distributed by brebook publishing software (www.brebook.com)

Julius Chambers, Julius Chambers, Julius Chambers

Missing

"In Sargasso."

MISSING

A ROMANCE

Narrative of Capt. Austin Clark, of the Tramp Steamer "Caribas," who, for two years, was a Captive among the Savage People of the Seaweed Sea.

BY

JULIUS CHAMBERS

AUTHOR OF "A MAD WORLD AND ITS PEOPLE," ETC., ETC., ETC.

MDCCCXCVI

THE TRANSATLANTIC PUBLISHING COMPANY

NEW YORK — LONDON

CONTENTS.

PREFACE.

Within a week's sail of New York is a vast and track-less waste, unexplored by the hardiest sailors, un-crossed by the stateliest ships; a monster mass of floating debris, consisting of growing seaweed, blooming and blossoming orchids, creeping and twining vines; trav-ersed by broad and easily navigated straits that stretch through its broad expanse of living green. It is called The Sargasso Sea.

There dwells a nation of castaways—a new and dis-tinct differentiation of the human race. Countless lost ships, whose tales of disaster never have been told, are floating there to-day. The destination of every wander-ing hulk, once it reaches the Gulf Stream or the Spanish Main, is this Harbor of Missing Ships!

Geographers have little to say about this floating con-tinent, but the Sargasso Sea has always been a wonder-shop to me, wherein are gathered all the lost, strayed and stolen treasures in the ocean's keeping. In every grassy cove, a story; in every watery lane, a romance; in every frowning hulk, a Secret of the Sea.   J. C.

MISSING.

CHAPTER I.

A KNIGHT-ERRANT OF THE SEA.

My name, with that of my crew of forty men, has been posted for two years at Lloyds in New York and London, followed by the single word "Missing." This statement is still true of the two score of good men who sailed with me in the steamer Caribas, but I have returned to New York alive.

I am an American, was born and raised in Brooklyn, and served my apprenticeship before the mast on the "Black Ball" line between New York and Liverpool.

I then entered the employment of Cameron & Co., at the age of 23, as second mate on one of the Australian ships, and made four voyages 'round the Horn to Melbourne. As we sailed on our return journey the last time I was made first mate, and, although only 27 years of age, an accident to the captain during the first week gave me command of the ship for the three months that succeeded.

On my arrival at New York I was offered a position as captain of a tramp steamer sent out from Plymouth by Triplett & Jones. That firm is one of the largest owners of vessels for charter in Great Britain. The little iron steamship was already in New York, and I went down to the Erie Basin to look her over. The Caribas, named after the Marquis of that name, was a trim craft. Her engines were of the newest pattern. She had no accommodations for carrying passengers, but her general fittings and equipment were excellent. The cabin and the captain's quarters were finished in mahogany; the forecastle was in hardwood, and very comfortable for the men. Although I had previously had a contempt for a tramp steamer and thought the command of such a craft unworthy of a deep-water sailor, I decided to accept this position, and to follow for a few years the wandering life it entailed.

There was some glamour attaching to the position, because, unlike the master of a transatlantic steamship, whose route is over the same course week after week, the commander of an ocean tramp visits all parts of the world. Entering port to deliver his cargo of goods to a consignee, he knows not whether a cable order awaiting him there will take him to the North Atlantic or the Indian Ocean, to Halifax or to Singapore. He must accept his duty in any climate; and the likelihood is that in the end his friends and employers will be watching the register at Lloyds, just as were mine through two long and lingering years.

The commander of a tramp steamer is a commercial knight-errant of the sea—a homeless wanderer, cut off from all ties of blood and affection, and devoted to the remorseless accumulation of gain for people personally unknown to him. His pay is always small, and the only opportunity he has of increasing it is by an occasional passenger from port to port, for whom he can surrender his stateroom and enjoy instead a sofa in the cabin.

Romantic as is his life, I never knew the commander of an ocean tramp who excelled at handling the English language. He may know how to box the compass, to calculate the latitude and longitude from the midday sun, to follow out the chart, or to work down a lee shore with the lead, but when it comes to writing, he usually lards his text with so many words only known to sailor men that the general reader is mystified and bored. While, modestly, I might claim a somewhat varied experience in the forecastle and the cabin, this is my first attempt at wielding a pen, and I shall rely very much upon the trusty blue pencil of the editor to render what I shall say creditable to me.

CHAPTER II.

MY FATAL CURIOSITY.

We sailed from Harbeck's Stores, New York harbor, on a fair June day, for the Azores, intending to make our first call at Horta, and then to touch at Ponte Delgada, whence we would proceed to Lisbon for orders.

At the last hour I had accepted a passenger in the person of Arthur Gray. He claimed to be an artist, and certainly exhibited evidences of his profession in the portfolio and drawing pads that made part of his luggage. He had with him one of the new Secor launches, propelled by direct explosion against the water astern. It was built with more shear than an ordinary craft of the kind, so that, as he maintained, it would be possible to navigate the ocean in calm weather.

Three days from New York, at Gray's urgent solicitation, I altered the course of the Caribas. After reaching longitude 40 I steered to the southeast and held that direction until the morning of the fifth day, when we began to sight many derelicts. My guest understood the purport of this quite as well as I did. He knew we were nearing the Sargasso Sea, that great assemblage of seaweed and floating hulks that for centuries has been accumulating in the eternal calm of the mid-Atlantic.

The gazetteers define the geographical limits of the Sargasso Sea as included between 22 degrees and 28 degrees north latitude and 25 degrees and 60 degrees longitude west of Greenwich. In area, therefore, it equals about 200,000 square miles, only slightly less than that occupied by the State of Texas. Its position varies somewhat from year to year, navigators maintaining that the floating continent, under the influence of a deflected African current, is brought several hundred miles nearer to the Azores some years than others.

I am not prepared to deny this, though I believe the extent of the change is exaggerated.

Being the navigating officer, as well as captain of the Caribas, I felt considerable responsibility in taking my vessel into this uncharted part of the Atlantic. The official Admiralty chart, as well as that supplied by our Navy Department, indicated open water in all that vast stretch between the Azores and Bermuda. But already large masses of floating sod, composed of matted and interlaced trees and seaweed, were within sight. I remembered the story of the ancient Argonauts, who sailed in the first tramp voyage to Colchis, and who encountered islands that "clapped together with the swell of the tide!" In the Sargasso Sea I found a veritable realization of that statement in the watery lanes that separated islands of seaweed. They were constantly varying in width. I was, naturally, very wary of penetrating any of these narrow sounds, for fear that the adjacent islands might close together and cut off my retreat.

A cast of the lead showed great depth. To anchor was impossible. I admit, however, that the thoughts of abandoned wealth to be found aboard the thousand floating craft of the Sargasso Sea appealed to my cupidity so strongly that, after a day's deliberation, I made fast to a great, rolling hulk that had once been a full-rigged ship. She was badly water-logged and had listed to an angle of 25 degrees.

The sun rose above the eastern horizon with great splendor on the following morning. The sky was clear and almost golden-hued. I was called on deck by the first mate because of the report from a man at the mast-

head, who had been sent aloft with a good glass to make
a survey of the surrounding ocean. The mate first
brought to my attention a wonderful mirage that appeared just above the horizon. I had never before observed a mirage in the eastern sky, and had supposed
that it was only possible for the setting sun to produce it.
But on this occasion all my experience was swept aside,
and we saw plainly in the sky an assemblage of vessels,
of all sizes and conditions, each separated by a narrow
strip of green sod, so arranged that they might not crash
together and destroy each other. The masts were still
standing on some, but in most cases these were utterly
gone. I cannot describe at this time the thrill of curiosity with which I scrutinized the strange discovery.
There was a semblance of order regarding the arrangement of the ships that promptly suggested to my active
imagination the presence of a directing human intelligence. But I said nothing to the mate on that subject.

We were joined at the bow by my passenger, Arthur
Gray, who was in an almost uncontrollable condition of
enthusiasm. He had been talking with the man from
the masthead, and added to our information the startling
declaration of the lookout that he had descried moving
objects in the City of Ships!

If I had been lukewarm before; if I had hesitated regarding the exploration of the mysterious region, my
mind was brought to an abrupt and decisive conclusion
by this statement. I ran up the rattlings to the masthead
and was greatly astonished at what I beheld. About
thirty miles to the southeast was clearly to be ·seen the
same congregation of vessels reflected in the sky and
already described by the man who had been aloft.

Then and there I resolved to accept the proposition
of Arthur Gray to enter his launch and go on a voyage
of exploration.

Committing the care of the Caribas to my first mate
and taking my quadrant, one of the ship's chronometers

and several days' provisions, I prepared to enter the launch as soon as it was ready.

A derrick was rigged from the foremast, and the stanch little craft was soon hoisted over the ship's side with the aid of a steam windlass. Meanwhile, all the oil tanks in the launch had been filled, and, adding a water cask, we were soon ready.

Fully expecting to return within forty-eight hours, I merely gave the first officer general directions regarding the care of the ship. I told him to keep the men employed with the tar bucket and the holy stone. On leaving I saluted the first mate.

The second mate stood at the ladder and touched his cap as I descended. He evidently had a premonition of coming trouble, and was so far guilty of a breach of discipline as to suggest that he be allowed to accompany me upon my hazardous journey. I replied with a frown and a shake of the head.

Without any suggestion from the owner of the launch, I took my seat at the tiller, while Gray looked after the engine. Despite the rigid discipline maintained aboard the Caribas, the entire ship's company, except those actually engaged in scrubbing the deck, assembled at the bulwarks to watch our departure. I confess that I was rather pleased than annoyed at this.

It touched my vanity, as I suppose it would have awakened that feeling in any man.

We got under headway about 9 o'clock and made for the first broad canal we discovered. While at the masthead I had attempted to follow this channel with my glass, just as I might have traced the sinuous windings of a sluggish stream through a grassy meadow; but I had not been able to outline its course beyond a few miles, because of the height of the brushwood, covered with its parasitic growth of plants. We steamed along gayly under full headway for about an hour, doing about eight miles, I should say, because of our heavy load, and although the channel we navigated varied greatly in width at places, it was broad enough at all points to have admitted the Caribas. The average width of the passage was about that of the Grand Canal at Venice, and though its convolutions were more numerous, we had no trouble in following the main channel.

As we penetrated farther and farther into this great mass of floating herbage, I was particularly struck with the strange mental effect produced upon me by the rise and fall of the ocean swell underneath the overlying mass. For the first time in my life I felt a sense of dizziness and seasickness. To the eye it was much the same as if in the midst of a far-reaching prairie one should find the land heaving and sinking in long undulations.

CHAPTER III.

I AM BETRAYED.

All this time I had kept close to my right hand a repeating rifle; but under the pretext of wishing to shoot some wild fowl, my companion gained possession of it and moved off to the bow of the boat. I thought nothing of this act for some time, but I observed that Gray always left the gun forward when he came amidships to attend to the engine.

When, at the end of three hours, we had come within plain sight of the great cluster of swaying hulks, and had reached a point where many small canals rediated from a central pool, my companion, the artist, promptly indicated the channel that I was to take and showed a familiarity with the landmarks that actually startled me. He would say: "Steer for that redwood tree on the port bow; bear 'round by that logwood trunk; keep wide out, and avoid the wire grass on the right just ahead; take care here, there's a sunken tree; put the helm hard down or we won't round this corner," and many other expressions indicating previous knowledge of the place.

I was on the point of asking him several times whether he knew or simply divined the obstructions, but I was so busy watching his movements, which now had aroused my suspicions, that I did not scrutinize the prospect ahead. For that reason we had approached within a short distance of the community of floating wrecks before I gave it careful survey.

Unslinging my glass, I focused it upon the first large vessel, and was startled to find objects moving about its decks. Uttering an exclamation of astonishment, I hailed my companion for an explanation. He burst into a hysterical laugh, but made no answer.

"What are they?" I asked. "Brownies or living people?"

"They are my countrymen!" was his reply, with an arrogance that was offensive to me.

My first thought was to reach for my Winchester and compel him to return to the Caribas; but the gun was in his possession.

A moment later the engine quit working—evidently due to some false adjustment by Gray. I also discovered that the oars I had placed in the boat for use in case of accident, had been dropped overboard, unobserved by me.

Though I had been brought up on the sea, knew no other life, and had passed through all sorts of dangers of calm and storm, I became imbued with an indescribable dread of my companion and of the strange people on the floating derelicts.

Carried by a current that I had not before observed, we were soon within hailing distance of a large hulk, and my companion gave a signal that was clearly recognized by the people on board.

Low as we were in the water, seated in the launch, I am sure that fully 500 vessels of all sizes, descriptions and conditions were in sight. Some of them were moss-grown. Others were covered with coats of barnacles inches in thickness. Many were bright and new as the day on which they left the ways and took their first plunge into the briny deep.

As we slowly drifted onward we were hailed from every ship we passed. The language was a weird and curious one, apparently a compound of all the modern tongues. All known languages of the world were represented.

Though my early education had been indifferent, exten-
sive travel had made me more or less familiar with Spanish, French, Italian, Portuguese, Norwegian, Russian,
German, Greek, Danish and, I may say, several dialects of
some of these languages.

Therefore I could follow the trend of the conversation between my companion and the Sargassons.

Their speech chiefly concerned me. Little by little I
became cognizant of the fact that I had been lured away
from my ship and into the hands of this strange people
by this pretended artist emissary of the Sargassons.
What the purpose of this kidnaping was did not at once
appear. I could not comprehend of what possible service I could be to this community. The few valuables
that I carried about my person, such as the Winchester
gun, my watch and diamond pin, could have little value
in their hands, because they had no occasions on which
to display articles of jewelry. I soon discovered that my
companion, the supposed artist, was well known throughout the community. He was hailed in a dozen different
tongues from as many different vessels, and always in a
respectful and familiar tone.

During all this time I had remained motionless at the
stern of the launch, deliberating upon some plan by
which I could get rid of my companion, and regain possession of the little craft, in which, by some miraculous
means, I hoped to be able to return to my ship. The
break-down of the machinery had, however, cut off that
possibility. Capture seemed inevitable, although I fully
realized that, had I possession of my Winchester gun,
with the belt full of cartridges that I still retained about
my waist, I could hold at bay the entire Sargasson nation. I reasoned at the time, and, as I afterwards ascertained, correctly, that powder was scarce among the Sargassons.

My first impulse had been to shoot my treacherous
companion with the revolver I carried in my hip pocket.

But I discovered that it did not contain a single loaded cartridge, and the recognition of that fact by my guard, who, from the bow of the boat, constantly kept me under cover with my own gun, increased his confidence and caused him to jeer at me. I therefore made the best of a bad situation and surrendered. I took one precaution, however, that was to secretly loosen the belt of cartridges from my waist and drop it into the sea.

A line made of twisted sea grass was finally thrown to Gray from one of the largest vessels, and we were soon drawn alongside. This hulk stood fully twenty-five feet out of water, and was imbedded in a thoroughly compact mass of floating verdure. As the boat was made fast to a narrow strip of sod and interlaced twigs that separated the vessel from the open water, my companion sprang out lightly upon a tree trunk, and, addressing me familiarly, said:

"We land here, captain."

There was nothing for me to do but to comply with his suggestion, and, making my way forward to the landing place, I sprang out of the boat as gayly as I could be expected to do under the circumstances. No sooner had my feet touched the mass of floating sod than I was made acquainted with a new and startling horror. I found the mass of tangled herbage alive with crawling insects, upon which large serpents, that abounded in great numbers, fed.

The trees that form a large portion of this garbage heap of the Atlantic are brought down from the upper Amazon during the tremendous freshets that prevail under the equator and are carried through from the Caribbean Sea and the gulf to the midocean swirl, where they reach their final haven. Their track throughout is along the current of the Gulf Stream, whose warm waters protect the animal life that happens to be upon the trees at the time they are carried out to sea. I afterwards learned that at one time marmosets from Brazil existed in considerable numbers in Sargasso, but the large serpents finally had exterminated them. I always had had a horror of snakes and lizards, and I therefore made haste to cross the quivering bog-holes leading directly to the water below.

My captor followed, encouraging me and directing me where to step in order to avoid mishaps. For the reason I have named, I gladly sprang up the ladder that had been constructed on the side of the ship as soon as I reached it.

At the ship's side, as I emerged above it, stood a man of unusually strange appearance. As I soon came to know him, he was the Kantoon of the particular communal family having its habitation on that ship. He was 60 years of age, with a grizzly gray beard, clipped or singed to an almost uniform length of three inches, that covered his face. His dress was made of what I afterwards discovered to be sun-tanned porpoise skin. His cap was of dark-brown leather, that had apparently done duty as a cushion cover. But I experienced another surprise when, on stepping over the gunwale to the deck, I found that the commander of the craft stood up to his knees in a tub of water!

The old man received me with dignified but gruff courtesy. His manner favorably impressed me. I reflected that, likely as not, my companion was an eccentric fellow, who thought to perpetrate a practical joke on me by pretending that he had brought me to this ship under guard and by force, and causing me to believe that I would be shot if I disobeyed him. My companion spoke to the Kantoon in Portuguese, and, having introduced me as the captain of the steamship Caribas, added:

"She is a fine boat, almost new, and would make a very desirable accession to our community."

This was the first suggestion I received of the thought that afterward became a terrible reality. Thus were confirmed all my fears, and thus was I made aware of

the cunningly contrived conspiracy by which I had been
lured from my ship in order that she might fall an easy
prey, by midnight surprise, to the heartless Sargassons.
Nothing that had happened filled me with such terror
as this information.   My mortification and danger were
enough to shatter the nerves of any man; but when I
fully realized, as I did within the first half day aboard
my prison-house, the tragic fate that awaited my companions, I was beside myself with rage and chagrin.

Meanwhile, I had been assigned to a small room that
apparently had been prepared for me amidships, just
under the deck.   It would have been a comfortable
enough place in which to have passed a few days in an
overcrowded vessel, but when I discovered that it was
closed by a heavy wooden door, with a strong bolt upon
the outer side, I understood that I was virtually a prisoner, and that at such times as I could not be kept under
the strictest surveillance I would be locked up.

The furnishings of the small cabin consisted of a bunk,
without any bed coverings, made of woven grass cloth
and stuffed with a pulpy seaweed that resembled the material from which our tapioca of commerce is made.   I
afterward found this bed comfortable enough, and, had
it not been that I was a prisoner, my quarters would have
been quite endurable.   Strangely enough, one or two
rude pictures adorned the walls.   They were either carvings in wood or had been burned into the oak partitions
with a hot iron years before the ship became a derelict.
Each carving or picture was evidently by a different
hand, and one of them, in my opinion, possessed considerable merit.   They reminded me of the drawings and
carvings upon the walls of the Tower of London in the
cells of the condemned.

They added another chill to my already drooping
spirits, and I concluded that escape from these unnatural
human monsters would be difficult.

CHAPTER IV.

THE PEOPLE OF THE SEA.

During the first afternoon I was allowed on deck for exercise I encountered my former companion, the pretended artist. He had laid away his store clothes, and was dressed in the garb of his adopted people. His feet were bare, and his knee breeches and jacket were made of shark's skin. His coat was laced together up the front like shoes, and fitted him tightly. His youthful face and long, curly, brown hair, combined with his costume, gave him a bizarre and interesting look.

I strode at once to his side and upbraided him in good Flatbush English for his contemptible treachery. He evinced neither regret nor humiliation, but smiled sarcastically and replied:

"We must grow. Take my advice and make the best of a mishap that might have come to any man who possessed the average amount of curiosity. In a few days we shall have your ship and most of your officers and crew under our control, and if you really think you will be lonely among us, our Chief Kantoon will make you the master of your own ship—after destroying her engines, of course, and twisting off her propeller, so that she can never escape from us."

"You mean to tell me, then, to my face," I hissed, "that your voyage with me was simply part of the scheme to obtain possession of the Caribas, and that you intend to add her to your infamous aggregation?"

Far from being displeased with my ferocity, the young
man appeared to be delighted.

"You will be able to restrain your feelings before long.
Life here is not so bad as you think. You will find our
government a rigid but not a burdensome one. Our
taxes are light and our social obligations are few."

"What is to become of my crew?" I demanded, still
chafing with rage.

"That is a matter that will have to be left entirely to
the Chief Kantoon, who dwells upon a ship at a distance
from here, in the interior of his floating nation. Some
time is required to reach his sacred community in a small
boat. It is a very tortuous and laborious trip to make,
through an intricate network of small canals, an inland
sea, like that of Japan, at the further side of which is
moored his floating palace. Good Sargasson commanders visit him once a year. I have never looked upon his
face but once. I am only a child of this people. I have
been among them for five years. I was making a voyage
from Bermuda to the Canary Islands in a schooner. I
was taken ill with smallpox. The heartless captain put
me in a small boat and set me adrift. I became deliri-
ous, then unconscious, and after several days was picked
up by the Sargassons, nursed back to life, and have been
their willing slave ever since. I owe my life to them."

"But what is to become of my officers and crew?" I
demanded.

Gray's manner changed entirely, and I had no occasion to complain of his frankness.

"Those taken alive," he began, "will be given the al-
ternative of assisting in the navigation of the ship to this
neighborhood, after which they must join our community, or suffer 'the mercy of extinction.' With the Sargassons there is only one way of insuring themselves
against the vindictiveness of the world. Nobody is ever
allowed to escape from here. Yes, I know what you are
thinking. You are about to retort that I was allowed

to revisit the United States. You are right in suggesting an explanation of my conduct."

"I certainly would like to know how you came to be sent to the United States to involve me in this terrible misfortune," I interrupted, with as much scorn as I could put into my voice. "I would not believe anything you may tell me, however. You are certainly a contemptible fellow, and I am surprised that even the 'Sargassons,' as you call them, could be induced to repose any confidence in you."

Without noticing my contemptuous language, Gray continued: "It was not until I had been put to the supreme test, which you will some day understand, that I was permitted to return to the United States. I went only after taking the most solemn and sacred oath that can be administered to a mortal. Besides, you must remember that I really owe my life to these people. They rescued me from inevitable death after my own countrymen, who were followers of my own religion and supposed to possess all the humanity that it inculcates, had abandoned me to the sea in a heartless and disgraceful manner. Their conduct to me on this occasion would have been sufficient, did nothing else draw me to this strange race, to link my fortune to theirs. I am a Sargasson, now, before everything else in the world. I have forsworn my country, my mother, my friendships; and my fidelity to the people of the Floating Continent could not be shaken by any blandishment or threats. You will some day, perhaps, understand what these ties are that attach me so strongly to a life that is unnatural and, until one is inured to it, uncomfortable. I sincerely hope that the time may come speedily when you will be fully reconciled to your destiny, and even experience emotions of gratitude to me for having been an instrument in the hands of The Grand Kantoon—who rules the sea, and the air, and whose missionary I was. At present I am sorry for you, because I know how wretchedly you feel. I am sorry for your friends and family at home, who will sorrow for you. But there are worse fates than yours. The span of life among us here is reasonably long. You possess a constitution of iron that has grown sturdy under stress of heavy weather, unremitting toil and unrequited zeal. Here your ability and your courage will find recognition, and no honor in the gift of the Sargassons is beyond your reach. Be advised, therefore, by me, the apparent cause of your present condition, and accept the inevitable, just as we all accept unwilling life at birth, and just as you must accept the inevitable fate of man, death."

To say that I was not impressed by the manner and the remarkable words of this glib rascal would be untrue. I turned upon my heel and left him.

Darkness set in, but, as I looked out over that strange assemblage of silent, swaying hulks, I nowhere saw a single light to cheer my eyes. Darkness was a delight to the Sargassons. I would have found companionship in a beacon or torch; but even that poor comfort was denied me. I was conducted to my prison cell, for such it was, and was locked up for the night.

I threw myself upon the bunk in the vain hope of being able to sleep, but for hours that boon was denied me. My heart was equally divided between my family at home and the crew of the good ship Caribas, that less than fifty miles distant was keeping its watch over my vessel, unconscious of impending danger. I condemned myself a thousand times from every imaginable point of view for my foolhardiness in accompanying a stranger on such a hazardous and unnecessary expedition. I conjured up in my mind a score of ways by which I could communicate with the first mate of my ship and apprise him of the mysterious and unexpected dangers that beset him. But all such plans had to be rejected.

With an aching heart, I finally fell into an uneasy slumber, filled with frightful dreams, in which death appeared in every imaginable and terrible form.

CHAPTER V.

SARGASSON MANNERS AND CUSTOMS.

I was awakened at sunrise by the sailor who had attended me before. He brought me a tin cup filled with a thick, brown decoction, intended to serve the purpose of coffee, and two biscuits from the store of supplies we had brought in the launch.

The drink was not palatable, but I soon discovered that it had a very exhilarating effect upon my system, and I afterward learned that it was made from the leaves and twigs of a small parasitic plant that grew upon the water and upon branches of the floating trees. It probably came from Brazil originally, but it was very prolific, and spread over a wide area of the Sargasson sod.

The Sargassons were scrupulously honest. Everything that I had contributed to the outfit of the launch, even to the smallest biscuit, was reserved for me. It was very fortunate that such was the case; otherwise, I do not think I would have survived the first few days, before I became accustomed to the peculiar food of this people.

As soon as I had drunk the coffee, or tea, my companion in the launch called to pay his respects. He opened the door of my prison cell with his own hands, and invited me to step out into the fresh air.

As I stood beside him I could scarcely control the rage I felt toward the fellow. I saw how slender and insignificant he was compared with me, and I could have strangled him in his tracks. He doubtless divined the

thought in my mind, and took an early opportunity to apprise me that the punishment for murder among the Sargassons was drowning in a horrible form. Half a dozen
strong men would seize the murderer and crowd him head
foremost into a barrel of water, holding him there, despite
his struggles, until he slowly suffocated.

After a few turns up and down the deck, we were
waited upon by the attendant sailor, and I was informed
that I was to have an audience with the Kantoon, or
commander, of the vessel. He made his habitation in
the captain's cabin; but I was instructed that he "would
be visible" upon the upper deck, astern, over his cabin,
and that I might approach him there.

My companion cautioned me especially against any
exhibition of temper. He declared that anger was utterly unrecognized among the Sargassons, and if I exhibited any ferocity, it would probably be mistaken for
madness, and I would forthwith be drowned without ceremony or hope of intervention on anybody's part.

So cautioned, I climbed the ladder and passed behind
a screen of flowering plants. These grew luxuriantly in
a row of boxes that resembled gun cases. The earth in
which they grew had been brought from the hold, where
it had been placed for ballast in some far-away port.

In the centre of the deck, standing in a barrel of water, was the Kantoon. His grizzly gray beard was carefully trimmed, and his leather cap rested upon his head in
a jaunty fashion. In his hand he held a large telescope,
with which, when I approached him, he was scanning the
distant horizon. I divined instantly that he was looking
in the direction of the Caribas; for, with the naked eye, I
was able to detect the presence of smoke in the western
sky.

I experienced a genuine emotion of hope. If my officers and crew only had sense enough to get up steam,
go to sea and abandon me, I would be glad. There
would remain some hope of rescue, and I would not suf-

fer the humiliation of having my ship fall into the hands
of a class of pirates more heartless than any I had ever
read about.

At this instant the Kantoon turned, and, seeing me,
said, with a grimace that was filled with chimpanzinity:
"Morning, Senor Captaine. Es usted very good,
aujourd'hui? Sitzen sie down."

"I thank you, captain, but I prefer to stand," was my
snappish reply.

"No me burla!" the Kantoon exclaimed, in an ill-tem-
pered voice, despite the statement of my instructor to
the contrary. "Quando, I say, 'Sitzen sie;' you squat!"

"But, captain"——

"Io sono the Kantoon de cette ship."

"But, Kantoon, I see no chair upon which to be
seated."

"Quel difference? Sit upon the deck."

I seated myself as gracefully as possible upon the
damp planks, curling my feet under me, a la Turc, and for
more than an hour the Kantoon and I conversed upon
general subjects relating to the sea.

He adhered to his horribly incongruous polyglot language. So far as I could make out, he actually spoke
no one language with even a show of correctness, but
his vocabulary of phrases and words from the Continental
languages and English was enormous. There was hardly
any thought that he could not express clearly in that way.
A keen ear and ready mind were required to follow him.

Above, I have indicated in a few brief sentences his
mode of speech. The Kantoon never hesitated a moment for a word. He selected them with reference to
the context. Gender, conjugation and declension were
things utterly unknown to his system of grammar. I
soon discovered that he knew more Portuguese and Spanish than any of the other languages, and accounted for
that on the ground that he had been associated with
Spanish sailors more than any others.

After a little time, I grew to a better understanding of the polyglot language. I recollected that I had attended a performance of the great Salvini in New York, in which I had heard "Hamlet" rendered in very much the same fashion as the Kantoon spoke to me. The members of the cast associated with the distinguished Italian tragedian knew only the English tongue, while Salvini spoke in Italian. It seemed a trifle incongruous to me, in far-away New York, to hear Hamlet give the "Instructions to the Players" in sonorous Italian—a language they did not understand. No experience is wasted in this world, and the recollection of that season of Anglo-Italian tragedly prepared me for conversation on the Happy Shark.

The Kantoon then proceeded to explain to me at great length the organization of the ship. Early in the interview he was kind enough to announce to me that when I had become tractable enough and thoroughly reconciled to being grafted upon the Sargasson family tree, he would give me a station on board ship and an attendant to wait upon me.

This was encouraging, but I could not drive from my mind the fate of my crew and the terrible calamity that overshadowed my ship. Therefore, I fear I did not listen as attentively as I should have done to the ethical history of the Sargassons, shuddering meanwhile at the thought that I would have plenty of time in which to make this study for myself.

I did, however, pay sufficient attention to glean the following brief outline of the Kantoon's narrative:

The Sargasson people date back more than three hundred years, the Kantoon explained. He believed that they had their origin in the loss of the Spanish Armada, when many of the great galleons, escaping the destruction that England intended for all, put to sea in a disabled condition, intending to go to the Spanish possessions in America, refit, and return laden with stores. They were caught in the Central Atlantic whirlpool and never could make their escape. The navigation of the sea at that time was very poorly understood, and many ships that left port with chivalrous ambitions landed in the Seaweed Sea, never to escape.

The Sargassons became a hardy race, growing in numbers by the accessions of new ships; but they did not assume the features of a social community until, early in the present century, a slave ship containing several hundred Africans—who had mutinied under the leadership of a former chief and, without any knowledge of the mariner's compass, had sailed almost into the heart of the Sargasson continent, bringing remnants of their families with them—swelled the population. The negro women who came in that ship intermarried with the Portuguese and Spaniards, developing in time a race quite similar to the lower types of the Mexican and Central American peoples.

Wars had followed among them for the possession of the Sacred Light and for the establishment of certain holy days. While they had no religion, as we understand it, they believed in a divine creator, called the Grand Kantoon, who ruled the sea and the sky. But, naturally, all tradition of the existence of dry land had vanished, and as one after another ships sank from decay or the overloading of barnacles, the Sargassons captured others in the possession of the different races, heartlessly destroying every vestige of the preceding community.

The life of a ship was found to be about fifty years.

These bloody encounters were crowded with horrors of the most indescribable character. The natural fear of death originally had inspired the most desperate attack and most stubborn defense. As no one knew at what hour a neighboring craft might show signs of dissolution, it behooved the commander of each vessel to be always on guard, ever alert to repel surprise. Mutiny was of rare occurrence. United by the tie of mutual

hopelessness, every member of each ship's company knew
his only safety lay in union and fidelity to its other members.

During the last fifty years, the Kantoon explained, a
pathetic and charming philosophy had prevailed among
the people of the floating continent. It was regarded as
a matter of social ethics that the fate of each ship's company was identified with the life of its own craft; that
the intrusion of strangers from other vessels was neither
sought nor permitted; that there should be no sort of
intercourse between the people of the various ships, except on the few sacred days in each year.

When the Kantoon of a ship was informed that his
vessel was gradually filling with water, and that all efforts
to stop the leak or save the hulk were fruitless, it became
his grave duty to call together the community over which
he presided, and, while they sang the death chant, to go to
the realms of a future life with resignation.

This religious idea solved a great many problems in
ethics that had previously given trouble among the Sargassons. It was especially sad to the young generation;
but the children accepted their fate with the same stolid
indifference as the grown people. Of course, it often
happened that a young girl or a sturdy lad, whose vitality
was great, rebelled at the Draconian law; but, as escape
was impossible, they rarely evinced any outward signs
of their rebellious spirits. If they did, they were seized
by subordinates of the ship, on the order of the Kantoon, and with a few yards of seagrass rope were firmly
lashed to some part of the ship, or to the heaviest article
that could be found on board. They then suffered the
humiliation of having exposed their weakness. In case
the vessel did not sink as soon as was expected, the fet-
tered prisoners were permitted to die of starvation. There
was no hope of pardon. If, by any chance, the leak were
repaired, they were tossed into the sea, bound hand and
foot, and became a prey to the sharks.

In a general way, the Kantoon, who had already taken a serious interest in my future, explained the origin and forms of the sacred ceremonies of his people. These will be dwelt upon in their place in the narrative.

Finally, motioning me to rise, the Kantoon clambered out of his official barrel of water and strode away to his cabin, without the formality of saying good-bye. I returned to prison of my own accord, and, the door being open, I pulled it shut.

I wished to be alone with my remorse.

I can say truthfully that, after this long conversation with the Kantoon, I felt more unhappy, more dissatisfied with my fate than before. I was so irrational and ill tempered that I berated all so-called explorers of the sea, like Cook, Magellan, Sir John Franklin, Sir Francis Drake and others, who only skimmed around the edges of the Atlantic and never penetrated this wilderness of water and grass, where they might have discovered something that would have been of interest and value to the world—that, too, after Columbus had discovered, located and named it for them!

When I thought of all the millions of treasure and the precious lives that had been wasted in the attempted and futile explorations of the Arctic regions, I felt that money and human life had been wantonly thrown away.

In this wretched state of mind I remained all the rest of the day. I have forgotten whether I was fed or not.

As darkness fell again upon the heaving meadows, I incidentally overheard a conversation just outside my door between two members of the ship's company that threw me into an agony of mind. One of the men spoke Spanish and the other French, but I readily understood them. The purport of their conversation was that the Caribas was to be taken by surprise that night and its officers and crew captured and destroyed.

No possibility existed of giving warning to my faithful fellows. The thought did suggest itself that I could possibly escape from my prison, secure one of the boats and reach the Caribas before the invaders. In my journeys around the ship, however, I had not seen any signs of small craft. To avoid any possibility of escape, my companion, Gray, had sent the Secor launch he owned to another part of the community—I knew not where.

In vain did I attempt to release myself from my prison cell, but I found that, in closing the door, the bolt had fallen on the outside, securely locking me in. Loud calls for my former companion, the cause of all my misery, and for the Kantoon himself, received no attention. My presence on the ship was ignored, and the silence throughout the entire vessel was ominous.

How I prayed for moonlight! I hoped that the approach of the pirates might be detected by at least one watchful man in my ship's company; but the sky overhead was full of clouds, and soon became as black as ink.

A heavy mist began to fall, and every condition seemed excellent for a night attack on the ill-fated Caribas.

CHAPTER VI.

ATTACK ON THE CARIBAS.

What worried me most, as I chafed under the restraint of my narrow quarters was the silence that everywhere existed. Even aboard the Happy Shark, where I was in prison, not a sound was to be heard that night. And yet I knew that the old hulk teemed with human life, and that active preparations were going on throughout the entire community for an attack upon my steamer that meant death to her officers and crew.

There was I, like a rat caught in a trap, unable to aid or give warning.

As before stated, the front of my cell was upon the main deck and faced a hatchway. Through the grated door of my prison I could see the sky, and I was suddenly made conscious of the fact that a bright red light had appeared to the southward.

Any man who has followed the sea for half his life, as I have, never fails to assure himself on the points of the compass. The first fair day in which the sun can be seen to rise and set will give him the data from which he can take his bearings in the absence of a compass.

This strange light that I saw far away to the southward took the form of an immense red ball, far up in the clouds. I did not know then, though I learned afterward, that this is what is known among the Sargassons as "The Sacred Fire."

As may be readily understood, the keeping of fire

aboard all the vessels would be impossible. Therefore, the use of fire is confined exclusively to one great iron hulk, from which everything inflammable has been removed, and which is moored far apart from the rest of the floating ships. The cooking for the entire community is done there, and once a month a crew from each cantonment makes a journey to procure a store of the supplies that are gathered and held in common.

No office among the Sargasson people is more highly honored than that of the Priest of the Sacred Fire, whose duty it is to see that the flame never dies out. There have been years, I am told, when neither matches nor flints were procurable, and when the extinction of the fire would have meant suffering and death to the entire population.

The Priest who is held responsible for the maintenance of this flame gives his life as a bond.

So great is his authority that he can command the Kantoon of any ship to furnish fuel, and, in emergency, assistance in keeping the fire aglow.

Twenty years before my capture, a derelict had drifted into the clutches of the Sargassons that contained a complete railroad locomotive. The parts of its engine were transferred, after great labor, to the iron hulk referred to. The locomotive's headlight, into the back of which a magnifying glass of strong intensity had been fitted, was placed over the glowing embers of the Sacred Fire, and threw a pillar of red light miles into the sky. On this night in question the rays from the reflector encountered a heavy cloud bank that hung high over the water, and combined in a red, spectral ember in the sky.

I then remembered that sailors had often spoken of a mysterious light that hovered over the Sargasso Sea; but if I had believed the stories I had accounted for the balls of fire as belonging to those strange natural phenomena described as "Will-o'-the-Wisp," and associated with damp meadows filled with decayed vegetable matter.

On this night, however, I fully understood the purport of the terrifying blood-red blotch in the sky!

I knew, instinctively, that it was a signal to the Sargassons to assemble at some point for the purpose of capturing the Caribas.

I felt the jar of footsteps on deck; but as shoes and boots were unknown, little noise was made by the stealthy tread of the ship's crew. I could hear lines of men ascending and descending the ladders not far from me, and I realized fully that the boats were being equipped.

In order to properly describe the events that occurred within the next twenty-four hours it will be necessary for me to rely upon information secured afterward from various sources.

I was not permitted to witness the attack upon my own ship, and for days all information regarding the terrible event was carefully kept from me. This was not done to lessen my mental sufferings. I can easily imagine that I was forgotten in the excitement, and probably I would have starved to death had it not been for the thoughtfulness of some one who during each night placed under my door a wicker dish of boiled seaweed, accompanied by two or more biscuits from the remainder of the scanty store brought by me in the launch. This was very little food for a hearty man, but I was grateful for the attention.

Although I had not seen any evidences of womankind about the ship, I instinctively divined femininity in this thoughtfulness. I detected, in the neat way the food was arranged upon the small piece of matting, the hand of a woman. I saw in the act more than mere perfunctory duty.

I felt that I had a friend on board the ship, all the more precious because unknown.

In my loneliness I gave myself up utterly to despair.

Without hope, without companionship, and, above all, without news regarding the result of the expedition that had been sent against the Caribas; weakened by poor food and driven to semi-madness by want of care, I passed as much of my time as possible in troubled sleep, in which I dreamed dreams and saw visions. I suffered a great deal from thirst, also, because the water with which I was supplied was evidently the product of the rainstorms, with an occasional ration of distilled water, brought, as I afterward ascertained, from the ship on which was the boiler of the old locomotive.

The water supply was the greatest of all the problems to the Sargassons. Fortunately, rains were frequent and the seasons of drought far apart. But there were times when the consumption of an extra pint of the fluid aboard each ship in one day would have meant suffering for weeks. The Kantoon of each vessel always kept the water butt in his own cabin, and guarded it more carefully than any of his other possessions.

On the fifth day after my capture the Kantoon of the Happy Shark presented himself at the door of my prison, opened it with a quick jerk, and asked me to come out. I was so weakened by my imprisonment that I was slow to obey.

When I did face him I saw that a fillet of fresh seaweed was bound about his temples, below one corner of which showed a ghastly wound, still fresh and bleeding.

With a wave of his hand he motioned me to follow him to the upper deck, where, recognizing my enfeebled condition, he directed me, still in the curious polyglotic language of his, to seat myself, while he, as before, climbed into his barrel of water. After a few preliminary remarks, and, indeed, a thoughtful expression of regret that during the period of excitement through which he had just passed my comfort had been neglected, he told me the terrible story of the capture of the Caribas.

In a prefatory way, I may state that the boats used

by this strange people are made of grass matting, stretched over a light framework of wood (in shape like the birch bark canoe of the American aborigine), covered inside and out with a gum made of fish scales and wholly impervious to water. Each boat will carry only two people, one in the bow and one in the stern, and is propelled with paddles shaped like tennis bats, strung with thongs made from the intestines of fish, interlaced so closely together as to afford resistance to the water. These boats are so light that a man can readily carry one upon his shoulder, and so quick are they in answering the paddle that the little cockle shells can be turned in their own length. In these the Sargassons surmount the heaviest waves; but in the canals of Sargasso nothing rougher than an ocean swell ever exists. If the sea runs "mountain high" outside, its force is broken by the great blanket of sod that for thousands of miles rests upon its surface. So light and buoyant are these small canoes, rarely exceeding nine feet in length, that if one of them is swamped, the two rowers, treading water at the bow and at the stern, lift the boat, bottom upward, above the surface, reverse it, and while one of the crew holds an end of the little craft, the other member climbs into his seat, and, paddle in hand, steadies the boat until his companion resumes his place. The Sargassons have no fear of an upset. Their paddles are lashed to the canoe with long thongs, as are all portable articles that they carry.

Having explained the character of the boats in which the expedition set out, I may now reproduce, in my own words, the Kantoon's narrative:

The flashing of the Sacred Light in the sky—the blood-red spot under the canopy of heaven that they had been expecting since morning—told the Sargassons the will of their Chief. They all understood that the Congress of the Kantoons had decided that the **Caribas must** be captured.

The ship was to be literally overrun with men, fully armed; and, after its capture, the Caribas was to be added to our commune.

From the treacherous passenger, Gray, who was the cause of all my misfortune, the exact number of officers and crew had been learned.

Mercifully did death come to those who encountered it, cutlass in hand, upon the deck of the ship!

The Chief Kantoon reviewed the fleet of small boats, each having two valiant men, selected from the various ships for their courage and fearlessness. The number of vessels represented was comparatively few, owing to the fact that two hundred men were supposed to be amply sufficient to effect the capture of forty on a night so favorable to the undertaking.

In a clear voice the Chief Kantoon gave directions for the attack. He described the route so perfectly that nobody could go amiss. He divided the flotilla into two wings, one of which was to leave the Grand Canal through a small shoot, and approach the Caribas from one end, while the other wing of the attacking party would proceed down the Canal and menace the vessel from the other. The plan was to lodge the two hundred men upon the abandoned hulk to which the Caribas was moored, and to which access could be readily found through its open ports. Having effected a lodgment there, the Sargassons would muster, and at a signal would swarm over the sides of the vessel before the crew of the Caribas had awakened to the danger of the situation.

Each man in the assaulting party was provided with deadly weapons.

But the most serious thing they carried, because unknown to the assailed, was a fine, impalpable dust, carried in a fish bladder, which was to be thrown in the faces of the crew. It is composed of a species of red pepper, analogous to the Tabasco berry, and is temporarily destructive to the eyesight, and especially noxious to the nostrils and lungs. With it was blended a powerful drug, having all the qualities of opium, extracted from a fungus, quite like sape, found growing upon the water-soaked tree-trunks. The almost instant effect of this drug was to produce unconsciousness. Blinded and staggering, the victims would fall an easy prey to the attacking party.

The Sargassons have a horror of shedding human blood. They care nothing for death themselves, and never hesitate to inflict it upon others. But they dislike to see blood flow, and prefer drowning to any other form of death—a very natural preference, because their whole existence is associated with the sea.

In addition to this terrible death-dealing powder, with which each member of the attacking party was provided, each man carried a weapon of iron or steel, ground to exceeding sharpness. Firearms are not in use among the Sargassons, and the only weapon of that kind in the attacking party was the Winchester gun I had carried, and in which still remained about half a dozen cartridges.

After the last word had been spoken by the Chief Kantoon, and the members of the storming party had received his injunction that no one of them must return unless the prize was secured, the Kantoon chief in rank took command and gave the order to proceed.

In double column, almost half a mile in length, the boats set out upon their journey. Not a word was spoken, and so silently did the boatmen manipulate their paddles, not even a ripple was heard above the swash of the ocean swell. At the head of the double column, by the side of the Kantoon in command, was Arthur Gray, who was expected to act as guide to the party. His was the only boat that contained three people, he being seated in the centre.

For some reason he was an object of suspicion and distrust, and the two men in his boat had received secret instructions, on the first evidence of treachery, to lasso him, bind him fast, capsize the boat, and save themselves by dragging their craft apart from him, so that he would drown.

The fifty miles were traversed in about eight hours, the speed being intentionally slow, in order that the men should not be fatigued prior to the moment of attack, at which time their best energies would be required.

When the mouth of the small canal was reached, into which the right division of the attacking party was to enter, a halt was called, and the canoes assembled in two great parks.

A boat was sent forward to reconnoitre, and after an hour's absence returned to say the Caribas was still moored to the wooden hulk; that absolute quiet reigned aboard the steamer, and that an approach could readily be made as planned, over the deck of the derelict.

I forgot to say that attending each division were two canoes, manned by Sargasson boys. It was their duty to gather up and look after the boats when the attacking party precipitately left them to climb upon the derelict. At the bow of each canoe was a long painter of sea-grass rope, which it was expected would be made fast to some object on the side of the ship, so as to retain the boat, but in case the canoes became detached, it would be the task of the attending canoe boys to chase it up and take charge of it.

In less than half an hour after the two divisions had separated in the Grand Canal, they had reassembled to the leeward of the great floating hulk to which the Caribas was made fast. The thick rope fenders that had been placed between the iron ship and the barnacle-covered hulk gave out a plaintive, wailing sound that would have fallen upon superstitious ears with dire effect.

The presence of the attacking party had not been suspected aboard the Caribas, for no sounds were heard except the tread of the officer on the bridge. The fires under the boilers had evidently been banked for almost twenty-four hours, and were very low. Scarcely any smoke escaped from the funnels, and no steam whatever.

The great iron ship, therefore, was as helpless as a log. As before stated, the wooden hulk of the dismasted full-rigged ship had listed to starboard about twenty-five degrees, owing to the shifting of its ballast. Instructions to the Sargasson assaulting party was that each boat's crew should in turn take its place upon the side of the vessel, each man holding on by the barnacles, and by the seams between the planks until the signal for the assault was given. This was the sounding of the Caribas' own bell, which, as every sailor knows, occurs at each half hour.

Seven bells had sounded on board the Caribas as the boarding party silently approached, and the officer of the watch had been heard to call out, "All is well!"

Every member of the attacking party had effected lodgment upon the upturned side of the great wooden hulk.

The boats had been gathered up and were in the possession of their keepers.

Everything was ready for the signal, which was fully due and momentarily expected,

CHAPTER VII.

THE AGONY OF SUSPENSE.

I may now quote the Kantoon's own words:
"Every moment's delay added to the anxiety of the
commander of the attacking party, because a sneeze from
any one of the two hundred men would have exposed our
presence," continued the Kantoon of the Happy Shark,
quite interested in his own narrative. As he grew more
animated and excited, however, his language became so
polyglot that, had I not possessed a wide range of
linguistic attainments, I certainly could not have followed him. For ordinary narrative, I found he preferred
Portuguese and Spanish; when he attempted bits of pa-
thos, he generally employed a horrible admixture of
French and Italian; his descriptions were chiefly in
broken English, larded with German adjectives and Russian verbs. A free translation of his narrative ran thus:
"Aboard the Caribas was one man who nearly defeated our expedition. He was the boatswain, a sturdy,
rugged fellow, who you doubtless remember; his strength
and courage will remain a tradition as long as the present generation of Sargassons lasts."
"Yes, indeed; I remember the poor fellow," I added,
solemnly.
"As we ascertained, after his capture, the boatswain
had been a deep water sailor on the Atlantic nearly all his
life, had many times approached our continent and had
heard from sailors many tales regarding its mysteries. He

had himself seen the Light in the Sky that hovered above the floating sod; but, like every superstitious sailor, he hardly credited in his own mind the stories he repeated and affected to believe. He had been on deck at the time the Sacred Light was flashed. He had seen it, had studied it carefully with a night glass, and had assured himself that the cone of light proceeded from some point near the surface of the water to the cloud bank in the sky! He knew, therefore, what the naked eye did not reveal, namely—that the blood-red spot in the sky was the result of a reflection of something on the water. He had been very anxious in his mind about the matter, and had made several efforts to obtain an interview with the first officer of the Caribas, who, in your absence, was in command of the ship. That gentleman was so swollen in importance by the temporary authority invested in him by your absence, however, that he would hold no intercourse with the boatswain. Had he done so, I have no doubt that the fires would have been raked and your steamer would have dropped away from the hulk, thus rendering her capture impossible."

"He has paid dearly for his arrogance," I interposed.

"The boatswain evidently suffered under a premonition of impending danger, though he had no idea it would come in human form," continued the Kantoon. "He was superstitious, and expected the trouble in some unholy shape. For that reason he purposely omitted sounding 'eight bells.' Instead, he personally descended to the fo'castle and roused the men of the next watch. We could hear the sailors coming on deck, muttering and cursing and declaring that 'eight bells' had not struck, and that therefore their time to get up had not arrived. We knew this as well as the men, and did not understand the reason any better than they. The boatswain's watch expired at 4 o'clock, but he was disinclined to go below, and, as we afterward knew to our cost, he remained on deck awake.

"With the information that we had received from

Gray regarding your ship's company, we expected to find about ten men on watch, including firemen, engineer, lookout, helmsman, and the officer on the bridge. The steward, cooks and waiters we thought to find asleep in their bunks, so that they might be tied up and thrown overboard without special trouble; but the forebodings of this officious boatswain well nigh defeated our plans.

"Practically, he had contrived to awake every member of the ship's company, so that when the assault was finally made on the order of our Commander, the shrill whistle of the boatswain rang out on the night air, calling the entire crew to quarters, and informing them that a boarding party was attacking. The language of the boatswain's whistle, though unknown to me, was familiar to every member of your crew, and right gallantly did they respond to it. Almost as quickly as I can recount the fact to you, did they swarm out of the fo'castle to the cabin, armed with cutlasses, marlin spikes and clubs.

"Our directions had been explicitly given, and, in brief, were: As soon as our men crossed the bulwarks twenty of them were to assemble under the bridge, where all prisoners were to be brought. The right wing of the boarding party was to assault the cabins of the acting captain, mate and chief engineer. The left wing of the boarding party was to storm the fo'castle, and, with a plentiful use of the Tabasco powder, to capture the men—knock them on the heads, if necessary to reduce them to subjection.

"Before this pretty scheme could be carried out, the boatswain had organized a defensive party of about a dozen men—some of them only half dressed as they came promptly from their bunks—had armed them, and had made an attack upon about fifty of us. We noticed one peculiarity about the members in this party. Each man had a moistened cloth about his mouth and nostrils, showing that the boatswain had heard of our methods of warfare. They entered the fray with their eyes almost closed, and it was without effect that we threw handfuls of the corrosive and stupefying dust in their faces. They slashed right and left in a way that endangered the success of our attack. Some of the other sailors, however, believing us to be supernatural figures, crouched whining and sobbing behind the water casks and the capstan. It was not until the mates, engineer, steward, cooks and waiters had been subdued and tied up that our entire force turned upon the heroic boatswain and his party.

"Our Commander rallied the men at the ship's side and addressed to them a few words. Even while he spoke your brave boatswain was at work with an axe chopping the cables that held your ship to the hulk. In a few moments more the Caribas would have been free! But our Commander promptly gave the order to advance, and the boatswain and his few companions were captured. The gallant fellow fought to the last, and was only overpowered by superiority of numbers.

"The discipline exercised by our Commander was admirable. Except a bottle of rum, which was standing in the captain's cabin, and which was appropriated at once by several of the men, I did not see a single article filched by any of our party. The commanding Kantoon in charge of the expedition at once posted a man at each companionway, and within ten minutes the entire ship was properly officered under his direction.

"Of course, the first problem was what should be done with the captives. Among our people only one harsh code obtains—'Dead men never talk;' and we have almost without exception given to each captive the mercy of extinction. After all, this is wisest. A man in captivity always chafes under restraint. Happiness is impossible. What pleasure can there be in a life of misery? However sweet existence may be, death that brings peace and repose is preferable. Such is the view that we Sargassons

take of the blessing of extinction.   We regard it as an act
of kindness to prevent misery.

"Our commander, therefore, decided that the entire
ship's company must die.   Your little cabin boy begged
very hard for his life, and it did seem a very cruel act to
cut him off in his youth; but conquerors cannot be swayed
by mere impulses of the heart, and the sweet-faced little
chap followed your second mate over the side of the
ship.   We did not put him in a sack, but tied his ankles
together, and, having attached a heavy weight to his waist,
we dropped him feet foremost into the sea.   I carry his
sad, tearful face in my mind yet.   Of course we made
quick work of the crew.   As a rule, we simply knocked
each man on the head with a marlin spike, to render him
insensible, and then tossed him overboard.

"But when we came to the boatswain, who had made
such a valiant defense, I personally went to the Commander and interceded for his life.   He was on the point
of granting my request, when it was suggested to him
by one of the other Kantoons that the man would prove
a very disagreeable white elephant on our hands; that
we would have to feed him and watch him for several
years.   That settled the fate of the boatswain.   I felt very
sorry, because a man of tried bravery is always a valuable
acquisition to a community; and, though this sturdy fellow
had killed more than a dozen of our party, we all felt the
greatest admiration and respect for him.

"I stepped to his side (for he had been allowed to
stand up, lashed to one of the davits that carried a lifeboat)
and conversed with him for several minutes.   He seemed
utterly indifferent to his fate, said not a word regarding
his impending death, but he asked, and even begged, that
the life of the poor little cabin boy be spared.   He did not
know, of course, that the poor child had already met his
fate.   He expressed considerable curiosity about our people; told me about having seen the Sacred Light; spoke of
the premonition of impending danger that he had expe-

rienced; repeated some of the tales that had been told him by Portuguese sailors regarding the Sargasso Sea, and expressed regret that he had not given these stories the serious consideration that his prese it misfortune clearly indicated he should have done. We were cut short in the midst of our conversation by the approach of the Commander, who said, in his brusque way:

"'Now, my man, how do you want to die?'

"'It doesn't make much difference to me,' the boatswain answered. 'At least, it will not an hour hence.'

"'True,' replied the commanding Kantoon; but there are all sorts of deaths. I'd recommend drowning. I may be prejudiced in its favor, but it's about the easiest form in which to take your medicine. Out of consideration for your courage, I'll have you drowned on deck, here, if I can find a barrel filled with water. But you must make your mind up in a few minutes. We can't fool with you all night.'

"'Very well,' replied the boatswain, indifferently. 'I suppose I had better take your advice. Suit your own convenience,' and he bowed, just as if receiving a command.

"The order was at once given, and the head was knocked out of an empty water cask. It was placed upright on the deck, and in three minutes it was filled with water—a line of bucket passers having been formed. There were some mutterings, many Sargassons protesting against all this trouble about one captive; but nobody dared openly to oppose the whim of the Commander.

"I went over and shook hands with the boatswain, as well as was possible under the circumstances, his wrists being tightly bound together. He gave my hand a firm, hearty pressure, and I then turned my back in order to avoid witnessing his last agonies.

"He was seized by six men, pitched head foremost into the water butt, and held there until life was extinct. His struggles were not violent, and he died with the complacency that could be expected of a man who was naturally a philosopher, and who regarded the end merely in the light of an incident. The poor fellow's body was then committed to the sea with considerable consideration. Thus ended a duty that to most people would be thought very disagreeable. Among the Sargassons, however, we feel no compunction at taking life. We regard existence as something unwillingly thrust upon us—the loss of which is of very little moment.

"While this scene had been enacting upon deck, a part of our men had been ordered to the furnaces, fires had been replenished with coal, and by daylight we had steam enough to get under way. If you will cast your eyes in that direction," continued the Kantoon, pointing off to the eastward, "you will see that your ship is safely moored in a berth, where she will remain until our good mother, the Sea, takes her in final and loving embrace. Perhaps you would care to use these glasses, with which no doubt, you are familiar," saying which the scoundrel had the audacity to hand me my own binoculars, taken from my own cabin.

Right here, however, I want to say that petty theft was unknown among the Sargassons. The very reason that my sea glasses were in the possession of the Kantoon of my ship was that they had been committed to his care in trust for me. I found the same thing to be true regarding my articles of jewelry, wearing apparel and even books in the library that contained my name. I may anticipate far enough to state that in due time I received all these things, none of them the worse for wear or misuse.

I took the glasses from the Kantoon's hand, and soon located the Caribas among the vast assemblage of vessels that swung with the ocean swell. She lay at least six miles away, but I was aided in my search by a fine film of smoke that still ascended from her funnels. The fires were dying out under her boilers, and in another day she would be as incapable of movement as the oldest water-logged craft in the community.

The effect upon me was very saddening, and, laying the glasses down upon the deck, I bowed my head and went back to my cabin, to brood over my misfortune and the disgrace that had come upon me.

The awful story that I had heard from the Kantoon greatly depressed me. Remembering the fairly courteous treatment that I had received at the hands of the Sargassons, I had hoped that a few of the ship's company would have been spared; I had rather anticipated that the engineers and the baby-faced child in the cabin would be suffered to live; but now all such hopes were dashed.

I was utterly alone among a savage and unnatural people, who set no store on life themselves, and could not be expected to respect mine. It was not improbable that at any hour I might receive the notification that I, too, was to be accorded the "mercy of extinction."

In this frame of mind I threw myself upon my cot and moaned myself into unconsciousness,

CHAPTER VIII.

FIDETTE.

I was aroused from my stupor by a voice whose accents I had not heard before. Its tone was tender and sympathetic, and instantly awakened in my heart the dormant love of life. Before looking in the direction of the doorway I knew I was in the presence of a friend—one who felt for me in my hour of dire despair.

The question of sex did not occur to me—so completely does misfortune destroy all the impulses of the human heart ordinarily aroused in the breast of a comparatively young man like myself in the presence of womankind. With no other thought than that of gratitude for a gentle word tenderly spoken, I raised my face from my hands and looked in the direction of the speaker.

Before me I beheld a creature so startlingly beautiful that I felt my senses leaving me at the apparition. She was a young girl, small in stature, but perfect in figure, with hazel-brown eyes, and her hair, radiant, reddish-brown in color, fell 'round her shoulders like a mantle. Her skin was aglow with health, and her smile disclosed a row of pearly teeth that glistened in the fading sunlight.

She was clad in a mantle of woven sea grass, of blue and gray, held together at her shoulders by sharks' teeth. This robe was belted at the waist by a leathern girdle, studded with shells of rainbow hues, and fell loosely about her figure, much as does the costume of the Greeks, as I have seen it worn at the Piraeus and on the islands of the Aegean Sea. Her feet were uncovered, and of dainty size. Her pretty arms were extended toward me in a winning, beseeching way. In her left hand was a sprig of green and waxen-leafed rhododendron, the Sargasson emblem, as I divined at once, of a tender of affection. In her right hand was a small wicker tray of berries, resembling the wintergreen in color and size.

I gazed spellbound upon the pretty, dainty creature, not daring to speak, for fear the illusion would end. She was so unreal, so unlike a thing of flesh and blood, so weirdly picturesque—she was a fay of the water world!

As she opened the door of my prison cell, she said, in Creole French:

"You must be faint and hungry, monsieur. Do eat these berries that I have gathered for you, and be refreshed. Come, I will take you where we may see the sun go down."

"I thank you very kindly," was my deferential reply. "Yours is the first friendly word I have received since my captivity."

"I know you have been unhappy, and for that reason have I come to cheer you," was the frank reply of the graceful girl, as with a smile she handed me the sprig of bay. "It is the custom of our people that all captives who suffer the punishment of living shall endure isolation for five long days and nights, that they may know mental wretchedness and reconcile themselves to Sargasson life."

After this the young woman led the way aft, along the main deck, to a pretty cabin, in which was a large port that gave upon the west. Through this broad aperture the setting sun, a mass of golden red, could be seen sinking into the sea.

By my inquiring looks, though not by words, I put the question many times to this brown-eyed creature as to her identity, and how she came to be upon the Happy Shark. She took the earliest occasion, therefore, to explain in simple manner and with graceful gestures, that she was the daughter of the ship's Kantoon; that her mother had been a captive, like myself "accorded the punishment of living," merely because her bright eyes and teeth had pleased the fancy of the master of the Happy Shark. The speaker had been born in Sargasso, and had never known aught of any other world. To her mother, who came from New Orleans, she owed the quaint French dialect that she spoke and the slight acquaintance with the English language that she afterward confessed.

The young girl's story of her mother's life was as romantic as a tale of fiction. She was the daughter of a place woman, that peculiar phase of social life existing nowhere else in America except in Louisiana. Though raised amid surroundings that were not entirely respectable, she was brought up a devoted member of the Church and at an early age placed in a school, where she remained for eight years. She was taught to sew and embroider; to play the harp and to sing. Because of her pretty face and graceful manners, she was encouraged in the coquette's art, and a bright and brilliant future was predicted for her. To the mortification of the good sisters, who specially charged themselves with the young girl's future, and for whom they hoped to make an eligible match, she escaped one night from her protectors, as was alleged by bribery of the concierge, and eloped with a dashing young swell of the Crescent City. He was the son of one of the few large sugar planters who had saved their fortunes out of the wreck of the civil war.

When the rebellion was seen to be inevitable, he had converted all his negroes and personal effects into money, which he had transferred to the care of his London bankers. The plantation, of course, could not be sold. But thousands of hogsheads of sugar and molasses in his warehouses were rapidly disposed of, and the proceeds forwarded from time to time to London. When the war came, he entered into it with fervor and rose to the rank of brigadier-general. Although wounded in several fights, he returned to his native city in safety.

His son, who had been a mere lad at the breaking out of the war, grew up a profligate. So entirely did he alienate his father's affection that on his parent's death the estate was left in such a condition that he could not lay his hands upon a single dollar. A stated income was however, paid him, and this he spent in the wildest dissipation. Getting into the hands of money-lenders, he had, at the time of this escapade, mortgaged his allowance for several years to come.

When the deluded woman found that she had joined her life to that of a worthless adventurer, who lived wholly upon his friends, and who found his only excitement at the gambling table, she was heartbroken; but she accepted her fate with the same resignation as does the faithful woman everywhere. It was not long until neglect was followed by abuse and insult; but, according to the daughter's narrative, the mother's fidelity to the man she had trusted never changed.

In the Summer of 1872, having raised some money, the daring young gambler decided to visit Saratoga, where, at that time, games of chance were openly conducted, in the hope that he could retrieve his fortune. Marie accompanied him. They left New Orleans in a small steamer bound for New York, and had a pleasant voyage for many days. One very dark night, however, a terrible storm arose, and it was announced that the steamer had sprung a leak. The fires were soon put out by the inflowing water, and when daylight came the vessel had become a helpless derelict, rolling in the trough of the sea. Every moment seemed the last. The sailors lost courage, expecting the water-logged craft to capsize and sink.

The poor little Creole woman, faint with fright and filled with an inborn terror of the sea, quietly slipped away to her stateroom, crawled into her bunk and cov-

ered her head, desiring to await death alone, and to meet
it in this less frightful form. Thus she lay for a day and
a night, apparently forgotten. And yet death came not.
Evidently the anger of the sea had subsided, and on the
second day, hungry and despairing, she crawled on deck
to find the entire ship deserted and she its sole occupant.
All the boats were gone—officers, crew and passengers
had departed, leaving her to her fate. She had been over-
looked; or, if considered at all, it had been assumed that
one of the seas that came aboard had carried her to a
watery grave.

It required little tax of memory to recall the loss of
the George Cornwall, Capt. Timothy Rogers, that had
sailed from New Orleans about the time described, never
to reach New York, and whose fate, beyond the discovery of one of her upturned boats, was never known.

The young girl at my side dwelt with graphic fullness
upon the months that her unfortunate, deserted mother
had passed alone aboard the derelict. Provisions were
plenty, and she did not suffer for food or drink. Vessels
were sighted many times, but none of them saw the signal of distress that she displayed. So wretched and hopeless seemed her position; so ever present was the prospect
of death, and so appalling was it to her, that she slept little
and ate only food enough to sustain life. Many times she
seriously contemplated casting herself into the sea in
order to end her misery.

Months passed. She kept no record of the flight
of time. Moonlight, darkness, fog, fair weather and
storm succeeded each other; but the moon mocked her,
and the sun and the fetid breath of the Gulf Stream
parched her throat. Even the stars lost that assurance of
companionship, recognized by every sailor of the ocean.

The forsaken woman, alone upon her rolling, log-like
vessel, never understood by what route she reached the
Seaweed Sea. Of course, my pretty informant, knowing
nothing of the geography of the North Atlantic, could

not even offer a surmise, and the probability is that the derelict, carrying its solitary passenger, skirted the eastern edge of the Gulf Stream until it reached the latitude of New York and the longitude of Cape Farewell, when it began a zigzag course that eventually landed it in Sargasso.

Contrary to theory, the derelicts did not pass around the Azore Islands and thence southward past the coast of Africa, but, just before they reach the path of the transatlantic steamers, they are deflected to the southeastward, and make their way slowly to the Graveyard of the Ocean—the Port of Missing Ships.

Coming on deck one morning, after fully five months of loneliness, the solitary woman was surprised to find that during the night, and under the influence of a strong current, the ship she inhabited had penetrated far into the heart of the meadow-like expanse. It had followed one of the large open waterways with which Sargasso abounds On all sides were to be seen the vessels of the Community. The Sargassons had detected the presence of the new derelict, and, almost simultaneously with the discovery by the passenger that the vessel had reached some sort of a haven, boats were seen putting out in every direction to effect a capture.

The customary law of salvage recognized among wreckers did not obtain, as the system of government was one of absolute communism. All goods were held in common, but the keenest rivalry did exist among the inhabitants of the various vessels regarding their ability as oarsmen, and the Chief Kantoon always awarded the most precious article aboard the captured vessel to the Kantoon of the first crew to reach the side of the derelict.

As happened on this occasion, the Kantoon of the Happy Shark was first on board, and his gallant companions swung over the derelict's side with drawn knives and cutlasses, prepared to destroy any survivors that might be on board. But when they were confronted solely by the pretty Creole woman, savage as were their hearts, all saluted her in their crude fashion.

Solitary as had been her life, she had never for a moment neglected her dress, and she was so daintily attired that these rude people, whose blood was as cold as that of the monsters of the sea, felt their faces glow with delight and admiration as they gazed upon the beautiful creature. Perhaps they may have felt a pang of remorse at the thought that their captive would have to suffer the usual penalty accorded to all such members of the race as came into their clutches.

In a few minutes, of course, the deck of the derelict swarmed with Sargassons, young and old. All gazed with rapt admiration upon the pretty captive.

In a bewildered fashion, she had seated herself at her favorite place upon the after deck, and awaited her fate in silence.

When the Kantoon, who, under the Chief Kantoon, ruled the immediate cantonments, arrived and took possession of the derelict in the name of his people, the condemnation of the captive was a matter of course.

She was sentenced to be sewed up in a sack, heavily weighted with irons, and tenderly dropped over the side of the ship into the sea.

It was the duty of her captor—that is, the Kantoon of the first crew to take possession of the ship—to acquaint her with her fate.

This sad mission fell to the lot of the master of the Happy Shark.

He delayed the transmission of the message until he should have claimed his right, as the captor of the vessel, to select the most valuable article as a trophy of his success.

When the Deputy Chief Kantoon had spoken and demanded of him his choice, the captain of the Happy Shark did not hesitate an instant, but approached the pretty captivé, took her hand, raised it to his lips, drew her to her feet, and, leading her forward, replied:

"She is my choice."

It is needless to say that nearly all the Kantoons of the other vessels promptly protested against any such departure from the recognized Sargasson code.

Death was the penalty for intruding into Sargasso, and it should be meted out with impartial justice to men and women alike. But the brave master of the Happy Shark stood on his rights.

In vain his confreres, who had rummaged about the ship, heaped up before him a score of telescopes, chronometers, sextants and massive silver dishes. He shook his head. His choice was made, and he demanded that the Deputy Chief Kantoon confirm it.

"Thus came my mother to this strange people, apart from all the world," added my pretty companion.

I looked into her face and saw that the golden-red of the setting sun had imparted such lustrous beauty to her eyes and cheeks as never was worn by woman before. Her voice, too, seemed more musical as she continued:

"The Deputy Chief Kantoon stepped to the side of the captive and her captor, and rejoined their hands, for in her shy timidity the trembling woman had released her fingers from the bearlike clutch of the rude though tender-hearted man. He next muttered some unintelligible words—and so they were married.

"After the ceremony was performed, all the members of the community present appeared to promptly acquiesce in the will of their chief. From among the collection of trinkets that had been gathered from staterooms and cabins, consisting of jewels, money and rich articles of women's apparel, each man chose a gift for the bride, presenting it in each case with a few words expressive of good wishes.

"The Kantoon of the Happy Shark—my father that was to be—returned in an ecstasy of joy to his vessel, established the mistress of his heart in the captain's cabin, and, within an hour appeared on deck cleanly shaven and wearing a cravat of variegated sea grass most becoming to his sere and yellow countenance."

The sun had gone to rest. He no longer watched me across the swaying meadow. No one stood by to inter-fere, and so welled my heart with gratitude to the com-panion by my side, that, waving sense or reason far aside, I clutched her in my arms and kissed her fervently.

So nearly akin to gratitude is love!

CHAPTER IX.

AN OLD MAN'S DARLING.

The Kantoon of the Happy Shark visited me again on the following morning. After the episode that closed the preceding chapter, his hazel-eyed daughter had left me with a burst of laughter that, far from indicating offense, encouraged me to hope that my rudeness was forgiven. As soon as she had gone, I returned to my cell and drew the door shut.

Pretty as this girl was, I realized there must be many suitors for her hand among all the brave and daring fellows who commanded the various vessels, and I foresaw all manner of complications for me in permitting myself to fall in love with this pretty sprite. Yet, you must remember, I was barely 28; I never had had sufficient leisure before to be in love, and I was willing to take a reasonable amount of risk, even among this semi-savage people, for the sake of winning the affections of such a strangely beautiful creature.

When, therefore, my master suddenly appeared before the door of my cell and opened it, I had a presentiment that something disagreeable was going to happen. Anger was apparent on his face. Every individual gray bristle in his beard stood on end, and he viciously chewed the bit of sea grass that he always carried in his mouth.

"S-o-o-o," he began, "you have ventured to make eyes at my little Shark? You have told her that her teeth are white. You have held her hand, and, by the Sacred Light, you've dared to kiss her!"

My astonishment was so great that I only stammered in reply: "Why, most gracious Kantoon, do you accuse me? Did the fair young lady make any such a charge?"

"She? She! Not at all," was the prompt retort. "But you were observed. My faithful cabin boy saw what happened, and reported to me. In punishment I shall separate you. In a few weeks I shall take possessio i of the Caribas, which, from that hour, will be my canton-ment. You will remain behind. You will become the executive of this sinking craft. You have yet about two years in your span of life before the incrusted barnacles carry the Happy Shark to the bottom. You shall never see Fidette again. She will go with me to the Caribas, and, although she was born and raised on this ship, she shall never visit here."

I hastened to explain, with as full a vocabulary as I possessed, that he had exaggerated the importance of the incident his cabin boy had witnessed. It was true that I kissed Fidette, but she was an angel, and the salute I gave her was a respectful tribute of homage to her beauty and her divine character. I assumed entirely the blame of the episode. I said nothing about the young lady's visit to my cell door, but led the Kantoon to believe that we had met for the first time at the cabin window, where we had gazed together upon the setting sun.

This seemed to placate him a little, and, handing me a piece of bulbous root to chew, the Kantoon continued:

"I knew this morning that something had happened to Fidette. She was in a condition of hysteria during most of the night. In her sleep she laughed and cried. I did not know what to make of it. I doubt if the cabin boy would have told me of your conduct had he not feared his little mistress was growing dangerously ill. So far as I know, it is the first time she has ever been in love. Possibly I am mistaken; for what does an old fool father know? She

is evidently smitten with you. That is natural; you are
not such a very bad-looking fellow, and you must possess
talent and ability to have risen, at your age, to the command of so fine a vessel as the Caribas. As she grows
older Fidette is certain to become more beautiful. Such
was the case with my poor wife. She was the prettiest
woman that ever lived."

The Kantoon then told the story of Fidette's mother
in a far less intelligible way than the young girl had
done, and described the critical moment in his life, when
he had demanded her as his choice of the prize goods
in the ship George Cornwall, with becoming modesty.
Many another man would have enlarged upon this incident, and made himself the hero of it. The Kantoon did
nothing of the kind. This impressed me in his favor.
Beginning with their life aboard the Happy Shark, the
Kantoon said:

"As you may imagine, I was immensely proud of
my pretty wife. She was by all odds the handsomest
woman in the entire Seaweed Sea. She was the latest
acquisition, also, from the outside world. She brought
us history up to date! She never tired of telling us about
a great war, extending over four years, that you had had
in the United States; and, as I belong to a warlike people,
every detail interested me. The episodes of that great
conflict have become as household words among this
ship's company. Down in the fo'castle only this morning, I heard the boatswain describing the charge at
Gettysburg of that brave young Southerner, Pickett. Of
course, the naval battles interested us most, and from the
lips of my dear companion we heard details of sea fights
that caused our blood to thrill.

"About two years after our marriage Fidette was born.
She was a bright child from her earliest youth. The
Chief Kantoon, at that time a very aged and distinguished
man, stood for her when she was christened by the Priest
of the Sacred Fire, and many presents, some of real util-

ity, were showered upon her. The education of this child
became the sole object of my wife's life. She taught her
with infinite pains the quaint French she spoke herself,
and read to her out of some of the few books I afterward
succeeded in obtaining from the library of the George
Cornwall. For my part, I cannot read any language.
As a boy, I spent my days and nights at sea, and never
had an opportunity to acquire even the most rudimentary
education.

"When the stock of clothing that my wife had
brought from the ship was exhausted, she it was who designed the pretty costumes, similar to that worn by
Fidette. It is peculiarly Sargasson. Nothing like it is
to be found anywhere else in the world.

"Fidette assimilated, naturally, with her surroundings.
She is very expert with the canoe paddle, and can climb
the ratlines of a ship with the facility of a tiger cat. Were
it not for her fear of sharks, which I encourage, I believe
she would spend most of her time in the water. What
makes her all the more precious to me is the fact that her
poor mother is dead. She contracted a fever and died
six months ago."

Moist as was the garb in which the Kantoon was
arrayed—for he had just climbed out his cask of
water to visit me—I beheld tears well up in his eyes in a
way that showed he tenderly cherished the memory of his
beautiful Creole wife. I have ever since thought that re-
awakened affection for the dead made easier my way to
his heart.

This brave Kantoon, who had faced death and the
treacherous enmity of all his associates for a pretty face,
was completely under the domination of Fidette. She
was the real commander of the Happy Shark; but she
was full of tact, and avoided asserting the power she un-
questionably possessed. Although the father scowled at
me many times during this interview, and others immediately succeeding it, his feelings soon softened to such a

degree that I was no longer imprisoned, and was consulted regarding the weather prospects and other matters
of dull routine about the ship.

Up to this time I have said almost nothing about
our own community aboard the Happy Shark. My excuse for this is the number of incidents that have succeeded each other during my first few days on board the
queer old craft. Indeed, it was not until I had received the
"freedom of the ship" that I was able to truly describe the
social organization. Including the Kantoon, his daughter, and its chief executive officers (who regulated hours
of sleep among the members of the various watches, by
day and night), there were eighty-five people aboard the
Happy Shark. Their duties may be chiefly described as
follows:

The Kantoon was the visible representative of the
chief power of the Sargassons. He was responsible for
the health and the good order on board his ship. His
authority was unlimited in emergencies—it extended
even to life and death.

When the situation was not critical, however, he was
expected to submit the question of the execution of a
member of his own crew to the Chief Kantoon. This
involved a respite of two days.

Indeed, among the entire people, there seemed to be
the utmost reverence and respect for the central power.

Although I veritably believe that the blood in the
veins of the Sargassons is cold instead of warm, there
were many features about their system of government
that showed a thoughtful respect for the feelings of an
unfortunate fellow man.

The Kantoon, therefore, was an autocrat whose acts
were subject to review. Although his authority was
absolute on board his own ship, owing to the very condition under which he enjoyed life, I did not witness any
exhibition of tyranny on the Happy Shark, or any of the
other vessels that formed the community.

The system of government was quite incongruous, I admit. It was inevitable that it should be so, because, although all property was nominally held in common, actually no member of a crew could appropriate a blade of sea-grass or a single dried Ogalla berry (a fruit quite like the mulberry, that grew plentifully and of which all Sargassons were very fond), without the consent of the Kantoon of his ship.

Again, the superiority of the Kantoon was emphasized by the fact that he was the only member of the ship's company who was allowed to have a wife. This law, I saw at once, militated against my future happiness, because it seemed impossible to hope that I could rise to the distinction of commanding one of the flotilla for many years to come. Meanwhile, some ambitious suitor, whose record for bravery was established, would claim Fidette as his prize.

This thought, probably, caused the young woman's father considerable anxiety.

I wondered if it had ever occurred to Fidette to worry about marriage. She must have known how poor were the chances of our future happiness. Apparently, she accepted life exactly as it came to her, never borrowed trouble, and had confidence in her own ability to shape events to suit herself possessed by few other women.

She was among a wild race, with all the instincts and impulses of an American girl, but she never for a moment had a thought of deserting her father or leaving the old home, made sacred by the memory of her dead mother.

Such was the position of the Kantoon of the Happy Shark, and his daughter Fidette. Such were the facts that confronted me.

The first mate was the executive officer of the ship. He was expected to see that the vessel was kept thoroughly moistened, in order that dry rot should not set in. The Sargassons had a horror of dryness. They were the most cleanly people living—taking frequent baths every day, and while on duty keeping their clothing constantly damp. During each watch, one of the crew was stationed at the rail and drew from the sea a pail of water from time to time, which he dashed over each of his comrades, including the officer of the deck. The Kantoon, I imagine, stood in a barrel of water because of the show of authority that it gave to the mind of the Sargassons.

Dry rot was a constantly menacing terror! It was insidious in its methods of attack; outwardly invisible, it could only be detected by frequent borings of the ship's hull.

To the prevention of dry rot and to checking the accumulation of barnacles upon the outside of the ship, the executive officer gave the strictest attention.

So far as I ever saw, the crews were thoroughly tractable. Not a member of any of them, during my stay, attempted to escape. True, they were rarely given an opportunity. The small wicker boats, in which they made their journeys from ship to ship, would not have been safe, under the best circumstances, outside the vast blanket of seaweed that prevented breakers from forming, and the water-logged hulks from rolling over.

Each derelict was a social organism in itself; but owing to the fact that life, at the very best, was uncertain among these communities, each floating village had a law of its own.

The vessels were liable to destruction during every storm—by collision with crafts of stronger build, by the ravages of time, or by an over-weighted accumulation of barnacles, that, growing rapidly in tropical waters, often literally drew the hulks to the bottom.

A case of this kind came under my notice. Not far from the Happy Shark I saw a small bark, the crew on which were obviously enjoying their last days of life.

Their vessel was weighted with barnacles up to her bowsprit. Tons of the calcareous accretions were visible, as
the hulk rose and fell in the water. This painful spectacle disclosed one of the apparently cruel phases of Sargasson life, for the Kantoon of our ship sternly prohibited sending relief to that sinking craft or the saving
of the community on board her. I repeatedly suggested
that it was inhuman to allow our neighbors to live in
such imminent peril of their lives, only to be ultimately
swallowed up; but the Kantoon sternly shook his head,
and declared that such was the law of the Sargassons
—and his polyglot language was almost as great an infliction as death; that the people on board the bark had
enjoyed their full span of life; that drowning would bring
the relief they coveted; that the end had little terrors
for them, because it brought to them the blessing of
eternal repose.

Repose is the conception of Sargasson excitement!
Death is repose; therefore, it is welcome.

The lives of the Sargassons are quite lethargic, but
they are clamorous for rest.

It would be impossible to point out all the incon-
sistencies in the religious beliefs of this people. Take,
for instance, their vague conception of heaven. Believing in extinction, as they universally did, they could have
had no logical use for any heaven; yet, they hoped to attain that place of felicity, after death, and thought it to
be an absolutely level country, covered to an even depth
of three feet with warm, refreshing water, in which all
the dwellers could wallow and walk eternally. But how
the departed spirits were to reach this abode of bliss, or
renew their spiritual existence after their primary extinction, I never found a Sargasson capable of explaining.

If the Sargassons were mentally befogged regarding
their theories of a future state and of eternal rewards
and punishments, they had a great many thoroughly practical observances respecting this life. Their principal

article of diet was seaweed, which they served in the form of a glutinous pudding, like farina. Fish, which were very plentiful, furnished their only solid food. If Victor Hugo's theory be true that fish creates and sustains brain tissue, the Sargassons ought to have been the most intellectual people in the world. They devoured fish in great quantities. It had always seemed a severe penance to me to be compelled to satisfy my hunger, on one day in the week, with fish, and when I found it provided as a steady article of food, my appetite soon rebelled. The seaweed stew was quite palatable, being naturally salted to the taste, but I never could become accustomed to the sundried fish.

The seaweed, collected in large quantities, was placed upon structures of lattice work resembling grape arbors, and was thoroughly dried. It was then picked over and the edible weeds selected.

As a people, the Sargassons did not smoke, but there were some experts among them who could roll a seaweed cigarette. I never attempted to smoke more than one of them, though I found it quite as good as the Virginia cheroot served in the Italian restaurants of New York.

The Sargassons were a temperate people, although they produced intoxication by drinking rain water, in which spars and old anchors had been soaked.

All crimes had their punishments. The abuse of a wife of a Kantoon by her husband was practically unknown; but when thoroughly authenticated upon the evidence of a third party, this crime was punished by the execution of the wife—the theory being that the culprit was more rebuked by taking from him the partner of his life, and compelling him to exist alone, than in any other way. As he coveted death, the infliction of that penalty upon the Kantoon would have been no punishment whatever. Like the unfortunate widows of India before the suttee was abolished, all wives so "extinguished" made no protest whatever, but in every instance recounted to me, went to their deaths joyfully, because of the unhappiness and remorse they believed their absence would bring to the widowers.

This real touch of femininity interested me very much.

The method of inflicting the sentence of death for crime was very curious. The hands and feet of the condemned were drawn together backward, so that the body took the form of a capital D. The man about to die was then affectionately kissed upon the forehead by all his comrades, and while the rest of the ship's company chanted a dirge, the two men most beloved by him tossed the condemned into the sea.

To fall overboard generally meant death, because rescue by any other ship was forbidden, and no derelict was allowed to take such an unfortunate on board. If the wretched man could not regain his own ship he submitted quietly to the inevitable end.

Death, which ends all in Sargasso, as elsewhere, was so familiar to these people that tokens of sorrow were never worn. They met it fearlessly and without protest, believing that when their bodies were committed to their beloved mother, the Sea, the joys of eternal rest began. Children were taught that mermaids met the sinking bodies and tenderly bore them to coral grottoes, where they rested forever in peace under the watchful guardianship of the Greatest of all Kantoons, who rules the universe as he does the Sargasso Sea, and who never more would summon them to duty or to care.

Of course, the Sargassons knew not care, but thought they did.

CHAPTER X.

COOKING FOR ALL.

Day by day the Kantoon's heart softened toward me. The performance of my executive duties about the ship occupied my mind, and assisted greatly in reconciling me to my enforced absence from my native land. The presence of Fidette had much more than all things else to do with my contentment of mind. One of the pleasantest of my daily tasks was to keep guard over her while she took her morning swim. Armed with a long pole, at the end of which was fixed a very large knife, ground to sharpness of both sides, I swung over the side of the ship upon a broad board, suspended much as is a painter's scaffolding. Upon this I walked back and forth, with the heavy spear poised in such a way that I could hurl it at a shark and prevent the endangering of my pretty sweetheart's life. A section of the sod twenty feet square had been hewn away at the side of the ship, disclosing beneath the clear, warm water of the mid-Atlantic. Into this bottomless tank Fidette would dive from the window of her stateroom. She usually spent an hour at her bath, and then, seizing a knotted rope, she would climb back into the vessel, and into the same window from which she had emerged.

Thus, for weeks, the monotonous routine of my life continued. I passed as much of my time in Fidette's company as possible. The Kantoon's threat had not been carried out. On several occasions we had dined together,

and, after the pretty Sargasson fashion, she had fed me
with her own fingers from a bowl of seaweed pudding.

An incident of importance about this time was my
visit to the great floating kitchen, to which I have here-
tofore referred. It is needless to say that I was not
trusted to make this journey until I had shown by my
conduct that I was wholly reconciled to my Sargasson
surroundings. The distance was not great, and, having
learned in my boyhood to wield the paddle with clever-
ness, I found no difficulty in performing my share of the
work.

Armed with a formal requisition from our Kantoon
for the week's supply of cooked food for the cantonment
of the Happy Shark, we set out. This demand was inscribed upon a tarpon's scale with a shark's tooth. The
character and the amounts of the supplies were to me
undecipherable, because of the peculiar hieroglyphics in
which they were written. We occupied the leading boat,
being accompanied by ten others, fully manned, in which
the week's supply of provisions would be brought back.

We set out at sunrise and pulled steadily along the
Grand Canal for two hours. This was a trip of great
interest to me. For the first time I enjoyed the opportunity of seeing the other ships of the floating community
close at hand, and of studying the faces of their inhabitants.

I had decided before we had passed a dozen ships
that our crew was in many ways superior to most of the
others, and that, if I had to spend the rest of my days
among the Sargassons, I had been quite fortunate in
landing upon the Happy Shark.

I felt very sad when we passed the Caribas. I
found her moored in a new slip, cut for her reception in
the floating debris. Several chains had been cast over the
bow and stern, attaching her to stumps and trees firmly
imbedded in the surrounding sod. I scrutinized the dear
old craft thoroughly. Nothing was changed about her.

It was a mere fancy, but I imagined that she knew me!

On her deck were strange faces, all bearing the stamp of the Sargasson race. I was curious to learn who was occupying my cabin and sleeping in my berth, but the man in the boat with me could not, or would not, impart any information.

We reached the kitchen ship about 11 o'clock, and I was soon on board.

I have seen many strange places afloat and ashore, but none so thoroughly novel as was that vessel. Its main deck contained a series of rude furnaces and ovens, about which fifty men busied themselves preparing the food for the floating city. The work must have been very warm in hot weather and very dangerous to health in the cold season. I visited the lower decks and witnessed the reception of the seaweed, its assortment into fuel and food, and studied every stage of its preparation for the messroom. The great problem on board that ship was the procurement of fresh water, with which the cooking, obviously, had to be done. Several large condensers were set up and ready for use, but I could not discover that fires had ever been built under them. Most of the fresh water was caught from the skies upon a great awning of shellacked matting suspended over the masts. This awning was concave in shape, exceeding the deck area of the vessel, and was capable of catching a great deal of water from the skies. As it rained every second or third day, and the downpour sometimes equaled an inch and a half to two inches in half an hour, as shown by the rain gauge, the great tanks in the centre of the hulk were constantly kept filled.

As a rule, the Sargassons ate only one meal a day. This was partaken of on each ship in two messes, one consisting of the crew and the other of the officers.

The Kantoon of the Happy Shark, respecting the fact that I had been the commander of the Caribas, always insisted upon my dining with his daughter, himself and first and second mates. The service was of the rudest possible character. All surrounded a large porridge dish, and each person helped himself or herself therefrom. When the number of persons about to dine exceeded five or six there were two bowls or more of this glutinous material. One fish was always regarded as a portion. The fish were laid upon the deck on the usual strip of matting, and each diner helped himself or herself.

As I have stated, fish formed a staple article of diet, and it was prepared very much as dried herrings are put up in the English seaport towns. Long rows of men were seen cleaning and dressing the fish, which were then placed in an oven, through which hot air from the furnaces passed. Thus they were slowly dried, like our dessicated fruits in the United States. The oil was rendered out, and found its way to a tank, where it was kept for greasing shark and porpoise leather.

In this floating kitchen I discovered an article of diet I had never before encountered. It was a sort of wild rice or wheat, that was boiled in the grain and then hastily dried. In this condition it would keep for years. I afterward became very fond of this food, and was surprised to learn that it was not liked on board the Happy Shark. It had the taste of parched corn, upon which I know the soldiers in our armies had sustained life for months together.

The equipment of the cook ship was kept up by details of men sent from time to time from the various communities. But some of the older men had grown very expert, and occasionally concocted special dishes for the Kantoon of the vessel from which they had been originally drafted, hoping in this way to ingratiate themselves with him.

For example, a most delicious soup was made from barnacles. A bucketful of these small shellfish would be scraped from the side of a vessel or from floating .ogs, carefuly washed and then boiled in several waters. In taste this soup was very much like rich clam broth. Of course, it was difficult to obtain hot, away from the cook ship, for the reason that fires were prohibited upon any of the other vessels. Yet this rule was often broken, as we shall see.

While I was inspecting the ship, our men were loading the fleet of boats that had accompanied us, and early in the afternoon our return journey began. After a long and laborious tug at the paddle we reached the Happy Shark, in the darkness, and were welcomed back with a wild, weird chant. In this the Kantoon joined, and, rising sweetly above all the singers, I readily distinguished the rich, musical voice of Fidette, welcoming me home again.

Where separation is so unusual, and, from the very necessity of circumstances, people are compelled to live in such close and constant association, absence of a day or more over the ship's side seems a much more important event than it otherwise would.

CHAPTER XI.

"MUSIC HATH CHARMS."

Fidette and I had a very pretty habit of climbing far out upon the bowsprit of the Happy Shark, although clearly under the observation of every man on deck, and sitting there for hours dangling our feet in the water among the anemones and jellyfish.

On the evening of my return we had taken our places as usual and were engaged in a serious conversation regarding our future.

In Sargasso, the prospective bride is rarely consulted regarding the date of the wedding. But I did not want the rule to be followed in Fidette's case. I realized that with her beauty, the commanding position of her father, and, above all, the discreet instructions she had received from her mother, Fidette had probably had other experiences of the heart before my lot was cast with hers.

On this evening, therefore, I determined to make the condition of my feelings toward Fidette perfectly clear, to assure her of my unbounded love, and, if possible, to get her to fix a day when we should be mated.

I began by asking her if she were entirely heart free, and was assured that such was the case.

"I did love once," Fidette said, looking me frankly in the eyes and taking my hand as she spoke. "The young man was the son of an exiled Portuguese marshal, and had been condemned to penal servitude in the Azores for some political crime. He made his escape in a small boat with his father, hoping to be picked up at sea. Their provisions were lost overboard. The poor father went crazy from hunger and thirst, and, throwing himself into the sea, was drowned. The son became unconscious, and, after drifting about for several days, his boat was captured and brought to Sargasso, where the stranger was adopted by one of the Kantoons."

"How was it that his life was spared?" I asked.

"Oh, his case was somewhat similar to yours. His life was not forfeited because he had not come with any purpose of conquest. His addition to our numbers was an accident, an entirely unsought incident in his life. He was very handsome, very tall and very dark."

"How did you meet each other?" I inquired, although I had no intention of becoming a jealous inquisitor.

"Do you notice that large space of open water on our right, about midway between this ship and the next one?"

"Yes, I do," was my reply. "I have often wondered why the sod has not covered it!"

"One of the finest vessels of our community floated there from the earliest period of my recollection until about six months before you came," continued Fidette, thoughtfully.

I now noticed that her face had taken on an expression of sadness I never had observed before.

"It was one of Sir John Franklin's ships, that had been abandoned in the north, had drifted southward until it was melted free from the encircling ice floe by the Gulf Stream, and found a haven here with us. This was long years before I came into the world, but I have heard the story from my dear mother's lips many times, and I remembered the ship very well. On the Royal George the stranger found an asylum. He was so quiet and reserved that he attracted no attention whatever in the community for several months. One day, however, he came from the Kantoon of his own ship to deliver an official communication to my father. I was seated just where we are now. Our eyes met. It was a case of love at first sight for both of us, and although we found no opportunity or pretext to speak on this occasion, I did not let the second visit, which occurred within a week, pass without affording him an excuse to address me. I presented him the sprig of bay in token of my admiration, and, although he did not understand its full purport, he graciously replied in Portuguese, conveying his thanks. I speak only French, and, therefore, was compelled to murmur my appreciation of his words in that language. The young man replied in French, and we stood chatting at this side of the companionway some little time. Fortunately, the visit of his executive officer to my father was of longer duration than usual. The young Portuguese carried back with him triumphantly the sprig of green, and that act was the cause of much grief to us and of his subsequent destruction. Unwittingly, I destroyed the very life that I was interested in perpetuating. But of that I will tell you later."

"What was his name?"

"Don Fernandex Otranto," replied Fidette. "He had been educated in Paris and at Heidelberg, and his German schooling was responsible for the fact that he was an expert performer upon the trombone. I had never heard of such an instrument, and never knew what form it took. But I know that it is very sonorous and loud, because on our sacred days he often played for me upon this pipe, while I sat here, as we sit now, listening in enraptured fashion to its notes. Many of the beautiful arias were familiar to me because they had been taught me by my pretty mother, who sang well and played the mandolin to perfection. It became a source of great joy to my heart to hear Fernandez play. I contrived to communicate this to him during his visit to our ship, and, after that, at nightfall, he always played a few bars from the national hymn of his beloved country. It became as the Angelus to me, for my mother had been a good Christian in her early days, and never overcame the inspiration that the sunset bell had had upon her in girlhood!"

"You told me that the sprig of bay given the visitor by you was the cause of dire disaster," I suggested. "How was that?"

"On the ship where he dwelt the Kantoon had a daughter older than myself, but deformed and homely," replied Fidette, slowly and solemnly. "She was a fright— not that I ever saw her, for, with the single exception of my visit to the Priest of the Sacred Fire to make my vows, I have never been a ship's length distant from the Happy Shark. But I know that she must have been homely. She conceived a violent passion for Fernandez, which I am sure he did not reciprocate. Of course, he could not prevent her loving him, could he?"

"Certainly not," I hastened to reply.

"Well, when he returned to the Goo-ge-Goo, or Green Octopod" (as the Royal George had been rechristened), "the miserable girl detected the sprig of bay that Fernandez still clutched in his hand. She said nothing, and, as the unfortunate young man did not then suspect her love for him, of course he was unaware that the token had roused her jealousy. She had him spied upon. She corrupted the executive officer of her father's ship, who always accompanied Fernandez on his official visits to my father, and as a result the fact of our meetings was made known, and, indeed, parts of our conversation were repeated to the vixenish creature. Our dreams of bliss, all the sweeter because our meetings were stolen, ended with a terrible catastrophe.

"One morning I arose with the sun, and, as was my custom, hurried upon deck and looked out to the northward toward Fernandez's ship. It had disappeared. The sea had swallowed it during the night. Not a trace remained or a sign that it had ever existed, beyond that space of open water you see before you! Far down, down, down, in the depths of the ocean sank the Green Octopod, with every soul on board of her. So, in the frankness of my heart, I have told you how I have loved and been loved."

There are mean traits latent in our natures. I am ashamed to say this pathetic tale did not evoke in my heart any disposition to give vent to tears. I felt no particular regret that the trombone player had gone to feed the fishes in the mid-Atlantic. Candidly, I had almost as much aversion for him as Fidette had confessed for the humpbacked girl who had stolen her lover from her, and who had undoubtedly scuttled the ship when she found she was going to lose him. What if he had escaped? Was he a good swimmer? Fidette didn't know. The very ethics of the Sargassons would prevent him from declaring himself to his former sweetheart. Brief as had been his stay among these people, he would know that to save his life would be regarded as an act of cowardice, for when one's ship had reached the end of its career every soul on board of her must die perforce. But, poor chap, he had been in love, and that excused anything.

Fidette's story of the first awakening of love in her heart had thrown us both into a very thoughtful mood. Now that I am calmer and look back upon the incident, I see how ridiculous was my assumption of heart-who'e superiority to her. Although I did not permit the truth to find place in my memory just at that time, I can now recollect more than half a dozen episodes in my early life wherein I was as badly smitten as poor Fidette had been.

I sat moodily gazing down into the water and watching Fidette's little pink feet toying with the jellyfish and the sea urchins. Her gaze was to the northward—toward but far beyond the spot at which had rested the dwelling place of her first lover. She was in a reverie. I watched her face closely, taking one of her dainty hands in both of mine, and, apparently unnoticed by her, pressing it to my lips. Hardly a breath of air was moving, and the indescribable silence of the Sargasso Sea hovered over us.

Suddenly Fidette's face became transfigured. The pupils of her dark eyes dilated, the rosy blush of joy suffused her cheeks. I detected the slightest possible stiffening of the neck and elevation of the chin. She was listening. She changed her gaze toward the westward, and fixed it there. Her lips slightly parted, then broke into a smile of inexpressible happinesss.

Gently she withdrew her hand from my grasp. She had forgotten my presence; now she intentionally ignored me.

Across the waste of water and drift came to my ears a sound so shudder-inspiring that I in turn forgot Fidette. It was unlike any of the strange noises sometimes heard in the wakeful watches of the Sargasson night, defying rational explanation. It was music—demon music! I, too, put my ears apeak, and I needed not to listen long to detect in slow and plaintiff measure the rhythm of the Portuguese national hymn.

Fidette's face told me the rest. Her first lover was alive.

The trombone player had escaped,

CHAPTER XII.

AGONY OF A JEALOUS HEART.

I always disliked the trombone.

Fidette remained in the same ecstatic, absent-minded condition until we separated—I to pass a most wretched and unhappy night.

Alone with my thoughts, I marveled at the complete possession that this pretty Sargasson girl had obtained of my heart, and realized that I must decide promptly whether I meant to continue the contest for her affection or surrender to an unknown and unseen rival. This latter proposition was too repugnant to be considered.

Evidently this Portuguese, this Fernandez, was unworthy of Fidette. By every token he ought to have been dead. If his vessel had been scuttled, as Fidette believed it had been, it was his duty to have gone down with the ship. If he were a brave man and worthy of a good girl's love, he would be dead; the very fact that he was still alive, and playing the infernal instrument, was proof positive that he was a cowardly fellow, unworthy of any woman's love.

This logic suited me down to the ocean's bed, for I had developed a violent aversion to this man, although I never had known of his existence prior to that night.

The serious problem with me, however, was—Did Fidette really love him?

A young girl manifests her affection for a man in such an unmistakable manner that even a child can read her thoughts and look into her heart. One does not have to go to the Sargasso Sea to understand what I

mean. In all ranks of society the maidenly heart is very
much alike, prior to the time that its possessor has learned
the art of dissembling.

Fidette had been in love before and was ingenuous
enough to confess and to confirm it by unfeigned exhibition of joy. Had she been an American city girl, she
probably might have affected an indifference upon the return to life of her former admirer—but she was simply a
natural woman. Too natural!

Ah, but her heart was au naturel? What a comfort
was that thought!

Tossing out a sleepless night, I was on deck at the
first appearance of dawn, and scanned the horizon to the
westward in search of the ship upon which the mysterious
trombone player had taken refuge. Not a vessel was in
sight! I reasoned with myself that perhaps we had been
deceived by our imaginations—that we had not heard the
music. Assuming that the man existed, that the trombone had ben played, we might have been the victims
of an echo, because there was no vessel to the westward!

My duties about the ship employed every moment of
my time until early afternoon. I then ventured to call
upon Fidette. She received me coldly. Her entire manner indicated that she was indifferent to any further at-
tentions from me.

Stunned by her reception, I had the audacity to taunt
her about her lover. I showed her the ill logic of his
being alive—developing the thought far more fully than
had been done above. In vehement words I abused the
fellow for being alive at all, declaring that it was his
bounden duty never to have reappeared in Fidette's path.

"If he be not a spook, or a Flying Dutchman, but a
man of flesh and blood who cares for you and respects
you, he would have boarded your father's vessel before
this time, in order that you might enjoy the pleasure of
seeing him again," I said jibingly.

"He would have done nothing of the sort," was Fidette's firm reply. "What do you know about our social customs? We are on the eve of the 'Week of Silence'— our great festival of the year. Fernandez and I must not meet until after the expiration of that gala period. Our minds would not be properly prepared for its joyous solemnities. But don't you worry; Fernandez shall dance the Bamboola with me at the end of the week."

Ah! but I did worry.

CHAPTER XIII.

"THE WEEK OF SILENCE."

The Sargasson method of taking rest was peculiar. Absolute inactivity was to them the wildest excitement. It represented their daily life of anxiety and the constant menace to death. On the other hand, dancing and carousing brought to them perfect rest.

The first day of the "Week of Silence" opened with a wildly hilarious dance, entitled "The Glorification of the Sun." In common with all the members of the Community, I was awakened at 3 o'clock. I dressed, and made my appearance upon the deck. There I found the entire ship's company drawn up in line, each man standing upon a mass of freshly gathered seaweed, stil damp with the ocean's brine. They all faced the east, where signs of the coming day already could be detected.

Just as soon as the great golden orb appeared above the horizon the ship's company broke into a hymn.

The music was in the minor key, and of a weird, monotonous character. The singing lasted for ten minutes, after which followed the Sun dance, in which everybody joined. It was somewhat after the fashion of the Roger de Coverley, and was accompanied by singing on the part of the dancers, that being the only music to which the feet of the dancers moved. The time was accentuated by the clapping of hands. A small wicker platter of shell-fish was then handed around, each person taking one of the scallops in his fingers and eating it. The dish was passed and repassed, and many times replenished, until all had heartily feasted. Then everybody was sent to quarters, and the sleep of one week began.

This sleep is to the Sargassons the supreme idea of excitement. It is indecorous to awaken until the Kantoon of the ship has himself arisen and summoned has cheif officers.

Fidette had not appeared during the morning ceremony. She watched the sun rise, however, from the window of her own cabin, and was thoroughly imbued with the spirit of the ceremony. She composed herself to rest contentedly, doubtless looking forward with cheerful anticipation to "Bantang," or the "Day of the Awakening," when her lover would be permitted to call upon her.

How I put in this wek of misery, I can hardly find words to describe. I was forbidden to move about the ship. Never having been a heavy sleeper, I awakened on the next morning and found that the Sargasson cook had very thoughtfully placed a dish of dried berries and baked fish at the door of my stateroom. This thoughtfulness I highly apreciated, because I knew that I would be very hungry. I carefuly divided the food into seven portions, in order that gluttony might not get the better of me, and cause me to suffer for the want of food later in the week.

I rose as usual with the sun on the following morning, and carefully tiptoed to the upper deck in order to make a long and thorough search of the horizon, in the hope that I may detecte the smoke of some passing vessel. I longed for the companionship of men who belonged to the real world that I feared I had left for ever. Although I climbed to the masthead, my search was in vain. Not a moving object was in sight!

I could and would have escaped had I not been in love with Fidette.

The description of one day will answer for all of those that succeeded during the week of misery. If the incident of the trombone player had not occurred when it did, I believe I could have occupied my mind during the entire week with thoughts of Fidette. But, under the circumstances, I was torn by jealousy, and my affection for the dear girl had been sorely weakened. Therefore, I used to sit for hours far out in the bowsprit, as it surged in and out the swaying sea, and rehearse to myself again and again the unhappy incident. There was an unreality about it that annoyed me. If Fernandez were dead some one else had played the trombone. Knowing nothing of Fernandez, this unknown would not come to see Fidette, and I could easily turn the girl's mind against the suppositious lover when he failed to put in an appearance.

She confidently expected me. Now, if he didn't come, I would win her!

I contrived to sleep about twelve hours out of the twenty-four. But the silence and the loneliness were very oppressive.

To me, of course, sleep did not mean excitement. In the long voyages I had made I had grown used to taking very little sleep. Besides, I was very anxious for Fidette to wake in order that we might be reconciled. Several times I contrived to look into her dainty cabin as I pased the half-open door, but she lay arrayed like a bride on her pretty couch, apparently in a stupor. The Sargassons never snore. I have been told that very few of them ever dream dreams.

Their lives are so romantic in themselves that they need no visions in their sleep.

Following my afternoon nap, I generally took a bath in Fidette's pond. She was asleep, and I did not therefore intrude upon her privileged property.

Almost counting the hours, the dreary week wore away. My provisions were entirely exhausted by the sixth night, economize as carefully as I could.

The seventh morning broke resplendently beautiful. The Kantoon, awakened, came bounding out his cabin with the skill of an acrobat, sprang into the air, and alighted neatly in the cask of water that stood awaiting him. It was one of my self-imposed duties of "The Week of Silence" to keep this cask filled with water. In the Sargasso Sea evaporation is so rapid that I have no doubt that the contents of the barrel would have been quite exhausted.

The magic of the Kantoon's voice awakened the entire ship's company. He gave a long, sonorous howl, which was the signal for everybody to start up and yawn.

A hearty meal was then served upon the upper deck, all being seated. Waiters were unknown, that idea never having developed in the Sargasson mind. The food had been cooked more than a week before and carefully stowed away in a water-tight chest, cast overboard to keep fresh, but held to the ship by a strong thong. One of the first acts of the steward was to drag this box out the water. Most of the men partook very sparingly. As for Fidette, she ate ravenously.

As I said before, I always liked the frankness of this young woman, for she never pretended to be anything but the ingenuous girl she was.

Then followed the closing event of "The Week of Silence," "The Dance of the Derelicts." This differed entirely in character from the "Sun Dance." The entire ship's company did not participate. All the sailors remained standing respectfully with bared heads while Fidette executed a difficult and rather tedious hornpipe. She was arrayed in a curious costume, the skirt of which was woven from variegated sea-grass, hardly reaching to the knees. The bodice was made wholly of tarpon scales, held together by some insoluble gum. How beautiful were her arms and shoulders! After the hornpipe followed a "walk around." Then, offering her hands to her father and the chief mate, the three skipped around the deck in a most hilarious "razzle-dazzle" manner.

Not a smile crossed any cheek during this ceremony, which the Sargassons regarded as wholly religious. "The

Dance of the Derelicts" is a public manifestation of gratitude to the Greatest of all the Kantoons for his mercy in permitting the Sargassons to have survived another year. It is not to be wondered at that this strange people are grateful for the protecting power of the Most High. They really appreciate the benefits that He confers in allowing them to live after their own manner and under their own laws.

To their way of thinking, there is a great deal of prosperity among the Sargassons, for which they are properly proud. They have no coin or medium of exchange, except sharks' teeth and tarpon scales, but these seem to serve the purpose very well.

The ceremonial ended as it had begun—with another feast.

Just as the long sleep throughout "The Week of Silence" had been to the Sargassons a continuous vision of the wildest excitement and a foretaste of the eternal bliss of the sweet-water heaven they all hoped to attain, so, antithetically, was "The Dance of the Derelicts," in which they found no pleasure whatever, a solemn reminder of the cares of this world.

Fidette showed no anxiety to see or to converse with me. The old love had supplanted the new.

On that night, in the silence of the midwatch, I eard the 'cursed trombone again!

"The Week of Silence" had only added to the vigor and strength of lung that the player exhibited.

I hoped that Fidette was asleep and would not hear her lover's signal.

I stole stealthily along the deck and looked over the ship's side, only to discover, as I had feared, Fidette's pretty head, with its loosened mass of dark hair falling in profusion about her bare shoulders, at her cabin window. I was glad that in the darkness I could not gaze upon her happy face and see again thereon that smile of ecstasy.

There was murder in my heart.

CHAPTER XIV.

THE KANTOON'S DISPLEASURE.

At an early hour the following morning the Happy Shark was put in shipshape for the reception of visitors. Several boats' crews had been sent during the night to the cook-ship, and had returned laden with provisions that were temptingly placed upon a large table on the upper deck; but neither the guests nor ourselves were expected to touch the food. The Sargassons ring a new change on the Barmecide's feast. Selfishness with them is a virtue. Charity begins at home.

Very soon strangers began to come on board. It was the one day in all the year when promiscuous visiting among the members of the communities was allowable. Of course, the Kantoon and the chief executive officers of the various ships visited and consulted with each other when occasion required; but each hulk was absolutely the castle of its commanding Kantoon, and he was at liberty to punish by death, if necessary, an intruder whose presence on board was personally distasteful to him.

My heart beat more easily as the long hours of the forenoon wore away without a visit from Fernandez. But, early in the afternoon, a small boat appeared on the Grand Canal, headed in our direction, and I instinctively felt that the oarsman in front was my hated rival. I was right. He came over the side of the ship in a jaunty manner, appearing quite indifferent about the character of his reception. He failed to send the customary bluefish scale to the Kantoon, required by the Sargasson social code. Whether this was a mere oversight or a bit of bravado on Fernandez's part I never knew.

It certainly gave mortal offense to Fidette's father.

Fernandez, however, did not seem to care whether he saw anybody or not, except Fidette. The welcome that he received from her was effusive to a degree that never could be equaled beyond the limits of the Seaweed Sea. She held the palms of her hands up to his face in order that he might kiss them, and, as he threw himself into a kneeling posture before her, she seized a large deck bucket, always filled with water, and emptied its contents over his head. The very highest type of courtesy took this form.

I was thrown into the deepest despondency, forgetting that I had always been a simple-minded man of the world, and that whatever seemed real to me in Sargasson life was absolutely unreal.

Fidette was dissembling!

I should have remembered that Fidette had never been effusive with me, and that what we call affection, the Sargassons regard as dislike. Deeply as Fidette's heart had been touched by the pathetic strains of the low-voiced trombone, the thought ever present to her that Fernandez had been willing to live when the blessing of extinction was vouchsafed to him brought a revulsion of feeling in the innocent young girl's heart.

Her public effusiveness ought to have shown me that she despised him! But I was so ignorant. In outliving his ship he had outlived her love, of course. If he had died Fidette would have cherished his memory for ever; but being alive, when he ought to have been dead, he was out of the court of love.

Ah! ignorance is never bliss.

During the long interview which the two young people had together I busied myself in other parts of the ship. I was conscious of the fact that the Kantoon was in a terrible rage, and that he had sent for his first officer, who, in turn, had summoned several of the most trusty men.

The visit of Fernandez came to an end. He was sent away with most affectionate handshakings and tender looks, these only serving as the signal for his destruction. The poor fellow walked on air, so happy had his welcome and tender leave-taking rendered him. He was exuberant in his manifestations of joy and pleasure. As he went over the side of the Happy Shark, to descend into the boat that he supposed awaited him, he stepped into a large sack, which hung suspended and open to receive him. The top was deftly gathered up and tied, and quicker than I can tell it the bag and its contents, heavily weighted, disappeared under the surface of the sea.

I never have approved of murder. But down in my heart I was glad there was one less trombone player, and that I had one less rival for the affection of Fidette.

An hour later the cruel little creature was sitting by my side in our old place upon the bowsprit, dangling her little pink feet in the water, and laughing as merrily as if her unfortunate lover did not rest at that moment at the bottom of the Sargasso Sea.

She assured me that her love for me was just as steadfast as ever. We wound our arms around each other like two sympathetic octopods.

And yet my thoughts constantly reverted to Fernandez.

How much art there is in having a woman throw you overboard at the right time!

The achievement is hers; the consolation—yours.

CHAPTER XV.

THE CHIN-GOONE REVOLT.

The act of the Kantoon of the Happy Shark in ordering the summary execution of my rival was equivalent to an acknowledgment of my acceptance as his son-in-law.

It was a shock to me that Fidette neither expressed any regret nor exhibited any remorse at the untimely fate of the Portuguese.

A round of strange ceremnoies then began, and continued for a month, during which time I had an opportunity of seeing all the Sargasson women. At a regular hour each afternoon they called in small groups to pay their respects to the prospective bride. I could not imagine how the information spread so rapidly among the communities. It seemed impossible that messengers could have been sent from ship to ship. I asked Fidette about it, and she explained that when a daughter of a Kantoon became engaged to be married notice was promptly sent to the Priest of the Sacred Fire, and the Sacred Light was flashed, signalizing the event. Every ship had a number, and was readily indicated.

But how was the news transmitted to the High Priest?

That was a mystery.

Not a single Sargasson woman came on board the Happy Shark that I did not see and carefully study. With-

out exception they were all undersized, though hardy
speciments of humanity. Their complexions were nearly
all dark, doubtless owing to their open-air life, and to the
fact that they never failed to exhibit their reverence for
the sun by passing a large part of each day, with uncovered heads, directly under his rays. I did not see any
woman who was as handsome as Fidette. But there
were many pretty faces among our visitors.

Their dress was most interesting to me. Sometimes it consisted merely of a few yards of sea-grass
cloth, tastefully draped about their figures. In other
cases the waists were made by gathering up a strip of the
same material at the neck and above the hips. The arms
were universally bare. Having no means of sewing, as
;we understand the term, the Sargasson women only
tied or pinned their garments together. In the association of the various primitive colors that the sea-grass
enabled them to employ they were very skillful.

There wasn't any national costume, but there seemed
to be uniformity about the dressing of the hair. I did
not observe any substantial variation from one form. The
women, young and old, wore their hair long, and twisted
it into a hard knot, directly on top of their heads, where
it was held in place by a few spines from the fin of the
shark. These made very satisfactory hairpins. In addition to these hair ornaments, the women frequently wore
one vertebra of the shark, highly polished and with its
appendant rib. I never understood the significance of
that adornment.

It would be unfair to describe any one type of Sargasson beauty. As I have said, nearly all were dark-
skinned, either from tan or by inheritance. I saw, however, two fair Greek girls who called at our ship, but I
was unable to learn from Fidette anything of their history, because she could not speak Greek, Turkish or Al-
banian, and the white-faced Greeks were not conversant
with the languages of Western Europe. These two

ladies were very becomingly dressed, and wore the only silk draperies that I saw during my stay in Sargasso. Their pretty bodies were wound in long, sleeveless garments, gathered at the wrist by a simple cord. They wore in their hair, instead of the customary shark bone, a sprig of sea myrtle, very shiny and waxen.

The ladies were received on board the Happy Shark with much ceremony. They were formally announced in each case; the fish scale of pinkish hue was sent to the daughter of the Kantoon, after which the guests were shown into the cabin and remained standing during the formal interview, when the congratulations were presented and acknowledged.

The entire party then seated themselves and began to gossip—and the women of Sargasso were certainly the peers of any of our American wives, sisters or mothers in that social art.

It must be remembered, in justice to them, that this was the only opportunity during many months when they could talk over their neighbors' affairs together. Every confidence poured into the ears of Fidette was dealt out to the other daughters of the Kantoons by her in turn, rapidly as the visitors came, strict regard being had to absolute truthfulness. The result was that little harm was done to anybody. It was demonstrated that truthful gossip does no injury. This chatter served to sustain mutual interest in each other. In most cases the gossip was utterly frivolous and harmless. This woman told Fidette about the illness of her cherished cray-fish; the next asked condolences upon the death of her pet octopus.

The octopus is the pug dog of the Sargasso! The young women affect and cultivate them as pets, much as our American girls do the hideous, black-nosed pug dog to which I have likened them. Indeed, the octopus is quite a companionable mollusk, once you understand him

No food was offered the visitors, the theory being

that food was provided in common, and each lady could readily obtain it on board her own ship. Many of the women had a fondness for schnapps, and inquired of Fidette if, in the capture of my ship, anything of the kind had been secured. They were always answered negatively.

One and all of the ladies, as they took their departure from the cabin were received on deck by a sturdy sailor, before whom they bowed their heads respectfully, and received the usual baptism of a bucket of sea water.

Drinking water, as I have explained, was caught in a tarpaulin roof that was constantly stretched across the deck. When a small cup of this pure liquid was handed to the visitor she was expected to take a sip of it, and then playfully to toss the contents into the face of her hostess, accompanying the graceful act with a gleeful shout of laughter. This was provocative of much merriment, and never gave offense.

If, during any of these visits, a rain storm came up, the ladies were never asked to remain on that account. Water had no terrors for them. Then, of course, in the canals of the Sargasso Sea, one had not·any great fear of the waves.

The only restriction put upon Sargasson femininity that I discovered was that a woman must not weigh over two hundred pounds. If she developed adipose tissue exceeding that amount she was unceremoniously drowned. Under such circumstances death was always willingly accepted by the ladies themselves. They had little fear of death at any time, but their repugnance to obesity was inborn; the old women all possessed anti-fat remedies, the formulae of which they imparted to their daughters early in their lives.

During this "Month of The Visitation" I one day noticed that the Kantoon's face bore evidence of anxiety. He believed he had detected spies upon his vessel, under the guise of visitors. He was right, because the fame of

Fidette's beauty had spread everywhere. Who had circulated the report? Naturally all statements made by visitors of her own sex pronounced her prim and homely. Already there were rumors of a social revolt against Fidette's right to be called the most beautiful woman in the Community. The gossips asserted that she was a treacherous, despicable girl; and one of the old dames even went so far as to declare that Fidette was a vampire, and had drunk the blood of her lover before his body had been thrown unto the sea. Indeed, there was no limit to the horrible things said about Fidette by the women of Sargasso.

Knowing Fidette's gentle character, despite the manner in which she had allowed her father to summarily dispose of the Portuguese trombone player, I gave no heed to the malicious tales put in circulation by the gossips of her own sex. I believed her to be gentle, pure and lovable. As our engagement was now acknowledged, Fidette insisted upon my saluting her with a kiss every time we encountered each other in public. She had a very cunning, and to me attractive, way of putting up her pouting face again and again, as she accompanied the act by saying "More!" and "Encore!"

The real cause of the Kantoon's anger toward Fernandez was not generally apparent, I admit; but eventually he took me into his confidence.

When I responded to his invitation to meet him upon the upper deck I found there, as a special mark of confidence and favor, a second barrel of sea water close beside the Kantoon's tub. Understanding at a glance the delicate character of the tribute paid me, I clambered into the cask without waiting to have it suggested to me, and we stood facing each other in our respective tubs for several hours, going over the offensive rumors that had been put in circulation by the Sargasson women, and that had finally reached the Kantoon's ears.

Then we discussed my future and Fidette's. With-

out attempting a reproduction of the polyglottic character
of the Kantoon's language, the following may be set
down:

In all frankness, he began, Fidette had made a mis-
take in preferring me to the Portuguese. The Kantoon
(Fidette's father) was the son of an Oporto sailing master. Fidette's mother, as we know, was a New Orleans
creole.

The propriety of the lover's taking off was not questioned for a moment. His life was forfeit by the Sargasson code. And yet, by these Sargasson people, the
trombone was held to be a sacred instrument, and this
young man had devoted his life to its study. It was
just their standard of music.

The Kantoon informed me that a rebellion was fo-
menting, the first that had occurred since the great Chin-
Goone outbreak in 1816, which grew out of a concerted
plot on the part of 200 Kantoons to organize an expedi
tion to go to St. Helena, rescue Napoleon and make him
the Emperor of Sargasso.

Napoleon was the only great figure in history thoroughly known and respected by the Sargassons. They
regarded him in much the same light as the ancient
Greeks and Romans did Hercules. To them he was
rather more God than man. His imperious and impul-
sive character filled them with the wildest admiration.

When these 200 Kantoons organized there was only
one fearless young commander, Chin-Goone, who stub-
bornly opposed the project. He did not want Sargasso
opened to the world. He defied the entire 200! Armed
with the only ship's auger in the community, at dead of
night he scuttled 100 ships occupied by the leaders of
the Napoleonic movement. These vessels, their Kantoons and their crews all went to the bottom.

The movement failed, and for one year this young
dare-devil Kantoon was, apparently, the most popular
man in all the Community. But he thoroughly under-

stood his fate under the Sargasson law. He knew that he must die on the anniversary of his act. He enjoyed himself as much as he could, and when the day arrived, accompanied by his hardy crew, he visited the stately vessel of the High Priest and submitted quietly and without resistance to being triced up and cast into the sea.

Recurring to the situation that confronted us now, the Kantoon was very grave, and said that the entire company of the vessel on which had dwelt Fidette's late lover, the Portuguese, had risen in rebellion because of the young man's execution.

They had secured the co-operation of twelve other crews, and a night attack for the abduction of Fidette and her summary punishment was highly probable.

The method of punishing a young woman who had been treacherous to her lover was quite peculiar. The false sweetheart was compelled to live, but lines of age and crows' feet were tattooed into her face. Her hair was bleached white, like an old woman's, and every vestige of her youth was destroyed.

Such an outrage, of course, the Kantoon was determined to prevent, and I was quite as resolutely opposed to it.

We agreed to double the watch, and to be prepared to take "boarders" at any moment.

Nights of sleepless anxiety followed.

I recollect that during the Virginius troubles we were beating down the Windward Channel one Winter's night on board the United States frigate Wabash. I was a member of the ship's company. We had been at sea for several weeks, and did not know whether or not war with Spain had been declared. Suddenly, in the moonlight, we made out a large Spanish man-of-war, about one mile off, on our starboard bow. The men were called to quarters. The decks were sanded down. The powder magazine was opened, and every gun on board was loaded with shell or solid shot. For half an hour, in the silence of the night, every man stood at his post, awaiting a signal to open fire. Even the surgeon had his knives, his saws and artery forceps ready on the ward-room table.

The great steel ship, that could have sunk our wooden craft in a minute's time, passed.

Not a sound on board! Not a moving light! Only silence—and suspense.

_____

The memory of that moonlight night in the Wind-ward Channel was renewed every night on board the Happy Shark.

CHAPTER XVI.

THE PAPIER-MACHE ORANGES.

During these days of harrowing suspense I saw much of Fidette.

Together we had walked into her father's cabin one afternoon and she was showing me its treasures. In an artistically designed hanging basket of woven sea grass I noticed a dozen or more orange-like spheroids, quite resembling the fruit in shape and color. I at first mistook them for the real thing, wondering whence they had come. But, on closer inspection, I recognized them as specimens of detonating bombs, manufactured in Wilmington, Del., and used upon the Fourth of July and other national holidays to add to the noise and the enthusiasm of the occasion.

They are fired from small mortars, and are hurled to a great height in the air. When their velocity is exhausted they explode. They are filled with charcoal and a fulminate similar to that with which percussion caps are charged. They are the most dangerous fireworks used, and the manufacturer will only sell them to the most experienced exhibitors.

A terrible experience enabled me to recognize these deadly missiles at a glance. Only a few years before I had been bound up the Delaware to Philadelphia for charter when the captain decided to anchor off Wilmington, owing to fog, and I, as first mate, was sent ashore to proceed to the Quaker City by train, in order to report

to our principals. I had succeeded in finding the mouth
of Brandywine Creek, and was rapidly ascending it
toward the nearest street to the railroad station, when, the
mist having lifted, I saw that I was near a large brick
factory at which fireworks were made. The exterior of
the building announced the fact and bore the name of
the company.

Just as I was passing this building, that faced the
little creek, a terrific explosion occurred within its walls.
The entire side of the structure was blown out, and one
unfortunate man was hurled almost over my head into
the water. Believing that I could render aid to the
wounded—and I was confident there must be many—
I told my men to land me at the little wharf near the
works, and hurried into the building. All was wreck
and confusion. Two dead women and five dead men lay
about the room. Almost without exception they were
unscarred and appeared to have died from concussion.
In a box, each carefully separated by a layer of cotton,
lay several hundred of these papier-mache-encased bombs.

They were exactly similar in color to those I saw
before me.

Evidently the Kantoon did not know the dangerous
character of the pretty yellow spheres that occupied so
prominent a place in his quarters. Just at this moment
the good man entered, and I asked him how they had
come into his possession.

Taking one up, playfully, he explained, as he tossed
it about from one hand to the other, that they had been
found in a box of wreckage that had floated into the canal
several months before, and had been picked up by one of
his boat crews. The box had been in the water several
months, but it was hermetically sealed.

"Oh! they are all right," he said, carelessly.

The Kantoon admitted that he had no idea to what
use the orange-hued spheres were put. He had been in
the habit of making ink from their contents, which Fi-

dette had used in decorating shells, fish scales and sharks' teeth.

I gently took the small sphere from the Kantoon's fingers and replaced it in the basket, telling him in a general way that harm might come to him if he dropped one. To Fidette, however, on the earliest opportunity, I made a free and frank confession. I told her that to drop one of those detonating shells meant instant death to every one within a radius of twenty-five feet. She appeared to attach no importance to my caution, but my words found an indelible place in her bright memory.

It was an episode that only a woman's genius could turn to future account.

They were to become "blood oranges."

The history of this revolt against the Kantoon of the Happy Shark, is exceedingly curious.

Ostensibly, the rebellion was for the purpose of avenging the death of the young Portuguese lover of Fidette. But it was led by a young man who had not personally known the Portuguese, and whose real motive I shall now explain.

I have already told what a sturdy race of men the Sargassons were. This was due to the cruel, but invariable, rule of destroying all weak children and of putting to death all young men who, having attained their growth, did not reach the height of six feet or more. When a young man attained the age of 21 he was summoned before the Kantoons of twenty-one ships, who assembled on an island of floating sod, and he was then carefully measured as to his height. The only question ever raised was whether the candidate so examined had attained his full growth. Instances had happened in which the young man had been kept under observation for several years, and then finally condemned. The penalty was death.

There were no jails in Sargasso where people who broke the laws could be locked up. You will remember

that I suffered a few days' confinement in a temporary
cage on the main deck of the Happy Shark. It is not
improbable that such a cell existed on all the ships. But
the difficulty of caring for prisoners and the impossibility
of banishment made it necessary to inflict the death penalty for nearly all infractions of the Sargasson social customs.

One of the most popular men in all the Seaweed Sea
was the son of a distinguished Kantoon, whose barnacle-
covered ship was not far distant from the Happy Shark.
He had just attained his majority, and at a council of
Kantoons, at which he had presented himself, it had been
decided that he was a full half inch under size. However
much he stretched his neck in the effort to elongate his
frame to the required six feet, the decision was against
him. Most decided in his opinion was the Kantoon of
my ship. He scouted the idea that the young man had
not attained his full stature. He ridiculed the assertion
of the candidate that he still suffered from growing pains,
and finally turned the tide against a popular movement
on the part of several other members of the council to
give the candidate another year's grace.

It is doubtful if this extension of time would have
proved of real benefit to the candidate, because he had
already done everything in his power to lengthen himself,
having hung by his arms for half a day at a time in order
to expand the knee and hip joints. The Kantoon of the
Happy Shark pronounced the final decree that the young
man must die.

Entirely contrary to custom, the condemned protested.

His firmness in the matter, his disinclination to accept death when it was decreed him, excited wonderment.
As usual in such cases, he had a week in which to take
leave of his friends, at the end of which time he was expected to present himself for execution.

During that interval he fomented the rebellion.

The women who had visited Fidette on the Happy
Shark had repeated and enlarged upon the cruel incident of the Portuguese's death. The young insurgent
leader caught up this act as one of injustice, and gathered around him a faithful band of fifty rebellious spirits
like himself. They seized a derelict that was occupied
only by a caretaker, fortified it and scorned the mandate
of the Grand Council.

Hansko Yap, as he was called, announced that the
purpose of himself and his followers was to avenge the
death of Fernandez. But the real motive was to humili-
ate the Kantoon of my ship for the manner in which
he had persisted in bringing about the sentence of death.
Spurred on by the courage of despair, the young leader
developed into a veritable Commander Cushing.

With utter fearlessness he prepared the most deadly
engine that could be sent against his adversaries. This
consisted of a large spar—the foremast of his own ship—
which was neatly tapered to a point, and this capped
with iron. The spar was eighty feet long, and as straight
as an arrow.

The method of attack was to use this spar as a battering ram to break holes through the assailed ships.
With entire indifference to the presence of sharks, forty
of the young men who had joined in the rebellion would
spring into the water, clasp the spar tightly under one
arm, and with the disengaged hand propel the floating
mast at a high rate of speed. Starting back a thousand
feet or more from the derelict they intended to assail, they
would bring their engine of destruction forward with a
rapid and regular stroke of great power until within five
feet of the vessel, when, at a signal from their leader, all
would dive. The crash was so great that the hull of a
wooden vessel was always broken in.

With iron steamers the damage was less serious, but
it was only a question of time and repetition when a seam
would open and the plates start apart. Being without

any means of stopping the inflow of water, the Sargassons of the doomed ship methodically prepared themselves for death, and stood upon the deck chanting their weird, funereal song until the ship gradually settled and took its final plunge.

Such had been the experience in the attacks upon all vessels prior to the assault on the Happy Shark.

Already this bold opponent of public order had sunk a dozen ships, and had caused it to be made known among the entire community that our craft must accept the same fate.

As the defense had been placed completely in my hands, I took the precaution of having twenty boats in the water ready to be manned and sent out at a moment's notice. In similar cases the oarsman took his place in the stern of the boat, while in the bow was a sailor armed with a very sharp knife. The defense, therefore, was likely to be very stubborn, because a score of semi-savages, armed with huge swords, would be able to make a very serious attack upon twice as many men swimming in water. Excepting a few men who were already in the boats, keeping them in order so that they could be promptly manned, the rest of the crew lay asleep upon the deck, all armed with spears or cutlasses, awaiting the boarding party,

CHAPTER XVII.

THE SPAR FIGHT.

I had the morning watch, usually uneventful. I was standing on the quarter-deck and scanning the Grand Canal with the utmost care. We had been told the mode of attack employed by the revolutionists—not that they had always used the spar, for on one occasion the fifty insurgents had swam to the side of a vessel, swarmed upon its deck like rats, massacred the officers and crew, scuttled the hulk and departed. We were alert.

Suddenly I descried a ripple on the surface of the Grand Canal. It might have been caused by a sea monster, and I confess that at first I did not attach much importance to the moving object.

At the end of a quarter of an hour, however, it had approached so closely that I could detect the almost submerged heads of the swimmers ranged along both sides of the floating spar.

I hurried to the main deck, where the crew lay asleep, and awaking each man assigned him to his post.

Only the bravest were given positions in the small boats, because, unequal as appeared the struggle between the men in the water, armed only with short daggers, and the members of our crew, wielding heavy cutlasses in the bows of the small boats, there was a terrible feature about the fight to which I have not referred.

The Sargassons were born swimmers. They never

went into the water without a weapon of some kind to defend themselves against sharks, and the Sargasson youth, with his double-edged knife, was more than able to cope with any one shark that might attack him. This savage monster of the sea, as is well known, turns belly upward before it seizes upon its prey. The mouth is located under the bottom of the jaw, and it cannot seize an object on the surface of the water without turning over. Taking advantage of this fact, the Sargasson swimmer waits until he sees the white belly of the shark in the water, when he dives resolutely and plunges the terrible knife into the vitals of his enemy. Of course, it occasionally happens that he miscalculates his distance, or the refraction of the water deceives him as to the exact location of the fish. In that case he pays the penalty of his miscalculation with his life. But the value of such experience with sharks makes the Sargasson a terrible enemy in the water.

By the time that the attacking party had arrived wi.hin twelve or fifteen hundred feet of our vessel the Kantoon had been awakened and relieved me of the command.

The boats were equipped, the paddles were in place, and the sailors with their cutlasses, crouching low in the narrow bows, were ready to do and die.

At the word of command our flotilla of sea-root canoes emerged in two divisions from behind the stern and bow of the Happy Shark. At a rapid rate our boa's advanced toward the moving spar, which had now turned and was headed directly for our ship. The voice of the commander of the attacking party could be distinctly heard as he gave orders to his men.

The spar was brought to a halt, the insurgent chief evidently deciding to accept battle in the open water. The mysterious feature to me was the remarkable faculty that the men in the water had of keeping their bodies almost completely submerged. When at rest they all turned upon their backs, merely exposing their nostrils, and one of their ears in order to hear the commands when given.

The bravery of our sailors could not be questioned. Under perfect discipline, the two divisions moved forward and simultaneously attacked the two lines of men on the sides of the spar. It seemed a matter of only a few seconds when each swimmer would be cut down and the contest ended. In fact, the fight seemed such an unequal one that I felt, though I dared not express, considerable sympathy for the misguided assailants.

My feelings were not shared by the Kantoon, who, the very moment that he saw the insurgents had decided to meet their adversaries in the middle of the Grand Canal, rather than at the vessel's side, bestirred himself about the ship, distributing arms to those of us remaining on board.

He handed me a long and very sharp sword with the injunction that he hoped I would know how to use it, for the occasion would probably arise at once.

I was completely mystified, but did not ask an explanation. Nothing could have seemed more improbable than that any of the swimmers would survive the assault of our boats.

This only emphasizes my ignorance of the methods of Sargasson warfare.

Ten of the boats could now be seen rapidly approaching each side of the floating spar as it lay motionless in the dark water. The head of only one swimmer, probably the commander, was visible; but I knew that there were forty strong, athletic bodies ranged along the sides of that one piece of timber. The director of our attack had formed the boats in two lines, and the order was given for a simultaneous attack from both sides of the floating mast.

Had it not been that the field of my glass was sufficiently large to take in the entire scene, I probably would have failed to detect a sudden commotion in the water surrounding the floating spar. The forty heads of the swimmers rose above the surface for a moment and then disappeared underneath the water.

This fact had a perceptible moral effect upon the men in the boats. They appeared to be seized with consternation. Several of the oarsmen ceased to paddle, and, without exception, the men with cutlasses rose up and craned their necks over the bows, apparently seeking some object in the dark water.

Our flotilla was in a state of utter confusion and demoralization. And well might its members be alarmed. The enemy was about to attack from under the water!

In another instant many of the canoes had been capsized and were filled with water. In less than a minute only two of our twenty boats were still afloat, and their occupants were paddling for life down the centre of the Grand Canal, in a direction apart from the ship.

In the water, a deadly hand-to-hand contest was in progress. A few of our men had effected lodgment on the floating spar, after the soft and tender bottoms of their boats had been ripped open by the diving Sargassons. But their respite from death was very short. They were set upon by the insurgents and slaughtered to a man.

The only members of our party left at the end of five minutes were the four men who had escaped in the two uninjured boats!

All the others had died, gallantly.

Through my glass I could see one poor fellow still clutching the spar in the agonies of death. He was ruthlessly stabbed, but it required the combined strength of two men of the enemy to disengage his arms from the spar.

Before we on board had recovered from the horror of this spectacle, the terrible steel-capped spar was under way, headed directly toward us.

Our defense had utterly failed!

Something must be done at once. It was impossible

to move the vessel. I recollected, during my imprisonment, to have slept upon a large rope fender. I sprang down the companionway, seized this in my arms, attached a cord to it and swung it over the side of the ship, about the point I expected the spar to strike.

Watching narrowly its approach, I shifted it so that the terrible blow of the spar was received directly in the centre of the coil of rope. Though the shock made the old ship quiver, no damage was done. The insurgent chief was very much nonplussed at the failure of the battering ram, and slowly withdrew the spar for a second attempt. The probability is that, had his full equipment of forty swimmers been behind that engine of assault, the fender would not have sufficed. But in the battle Hansko Yap had lost eleven men, for I was only able to count twenty-nine heads in the water.

Onward, again, came the plucky and determined enemy. They swam with greater force, and the blow produced far more of a shock than the previous one; but I was able to interpose the fender again, and this destroyed its damaging effects.

Quicker than I can recount it, however, members of the attacking party began to swarm on board the Happy Shark, over the bows and through the stern windows, fighting desperately, hand to hand. They appeared to have only one object of attack, and that was the Kantoon. By a preconcerted arrangement they formed in a hollow square in the middle of the deck, thus separating our sailors who were forward from those aft, and moved rapidly toward Fidette's cabin.

At this moment the old Kantoon showed the stuff of which he was made. He sprang down from the quarterdeck, cutlass in hand, and slashed about him in a way that would have pleased the Three Musketeers. He cut down two men with his own hand before my eyes. One of these fellows, however, was not killed, and crawled along the deck until he reached a point where he could strike. He then literally hobbled the Kanroon by slashing him across the calves of his legs, and the brave old man, falling to the deck in a heap, was done to death in an instant.

The command of the ship then devolved upon me, but before I could have rallied the men we would have been defeated had not Fidette performed one of the most remarkable acts of heroism imaginable.

CHAPTER XVIII.
FRUIT FOR DEAD MEN.

Among the Sargassons quarter is never asked or given.

The enemy were in possession of our upper deck, and had formed in a hollow square around the main hatchway, leading below. Prior to the engagement, a cover had been placed upon this hatch and securely fastened. Otherwise, some of the enemy would have been sent below to cut the throats of our wounded as they lay in the sick bay.

I was on the quarter deck, and recognized the extreme gravity of the situation.

Although I had passed through many critical moments during my long and active career as a sailor and commander, I never felt the absolute imminence of death so keenly. I realized that I must meet my end bravely, but I confess that the thought that I must virtually compel one of these savage brutes to carve me to pieces, still alive, with the terrible double-edged knife that he carried in his hands, was not pleasing.

Every man on board knew that there was no hope of saving his life by surrender.

Earlier in the fight, Fidette had rushed to my side, and declared that if I thought the ship could be saved by her surrender, she would willingly give herself up. Naturally, such a suggestion was utterly repugnant to me, and I had rejected it.

The few brave fellows around me regarded the situation far more complacently than did I. Their breasts did not seem to be torn with the agony that lacerated mine. They viewed the approaching extinction as a mere incident, while to me it appeared the horrible crisis that it is to most men of our race. Besides, I had accepted the care of Fidette's life, and was burdened with a responsibility that none of my companions shared.

As we stood there, prepared for a final and hopeless defense, we felt that within a quarter of an hour those of us who escaped the horrible knives of our assailants would be lashed to some part of the rigging and sent to the bottom of the sea with our scuttled ship.

I had sent Fidette to her cabin with the solemn injunction that she must be prepared for death. She proved to be a very brave and heroic little woman. She bade me farewell in a tender and affectionate manner, wholly different from the well-remembered parting with the trombone player, as he went over the side of the ship to a death that she knew was prepared for him. I felt that I detected real affection in the playful twist she gave to a lock of my hair that hung down over my forehead.

Every man's experience fits his own vanity!

I had not forgotten the dear girl, however, and, racked as was my heart with conflicting emotions, I saw her, in my fancy, seated in her cabin, awaiting her doom.

There was only six of us on the quarter deck, but we were determined to sell our lives as dearly as possible. The rest of the ship's company, many of them being unarmed, were huddled together at the bow of the vessel. We all carried heavy cutlasses, and had some sort of a chance for defense, while the poor fellows forward meekly awaited death, without hope of resistance.

We could see that the leader of the enemy was instructing his men. He pointed to us in turn, evidently assigning two of his assassins to each man. We were awaiting the onslaught with nerves at the highest tension, when suddenly I observed the eyes of our enemies moving in the direction of the starboard quarter. Something had diverted their attention from the vital instructions of their commander.

Turning my head, I saw my pretty Fidette, arrayed in her newest and brightest sea-grass, shell-bespangled dress, creeping above the gunwale of the ship, evidently from the window of her cabin. There was a sweet and gentle smile upon her face. Her long tresses, carefully combed out, streamed in the air. With all the agility of a cat, she sprang to the top of the rail and hurried forward to the standing rigging.

I saw that she carried on the side away from the enemy's view, the little wicker basket filled with the pretty orange-hued bombs!

Was she determined upon self-destruction?

I sprang forward in the hope of stopping her, as I expected to see her blown to atoms. Without looking in my direction, however, she bounded toward the ladder, and quicker than I can say it her little bare feet were climbing the worn and broken rattlings.

Then I understood the meaning of her actions! She was about to ascend to the masthead, whence she evidently intended to hurl the bombs upon the enemy below.

I watched her with bated breath, fearing that she might fall to the deck. I knew how rotten and treacherous was the disused rigging. Clearly, nobody besides myself comprehended her purpose. Twice she nearly fell. Again and again the tarred ropes broke beneath her feet. But she was firm of purpose and rapidly neared the top.

How can I pay tribute to her conduct? How can I cause the reader to feel the boundless emotions of pride that stirred my bosom at such a moment?

I forgave her everything—even the trombone man, even her lack of sympathy and the frivolity of her character.

A moment! Now she was at the masthead! The

crisis was at hand! The men who formed the hollow square on the deck below had not taken their eyes from the climbing figure. It is doubtful if they had not mistaken the little wicker basket on her arm for a hat.

I enjoyed her triumph. I knew she was mistress of the situation. She held the power of life and death over all of us.

She waved her hand to the men about to die. She gave a jaunty toss of her head in my direction.

Our enemies were charmed as by a magic spell. Fidette softened their hearts—hearts steeled against all human emotions.

She appealed to another and very different passion than the desire for blood.

She stole murder from their hearts, and planted love there instead. Her charms seduced them, even as her beautiful hand was about to slay them.

It was well that it was so; for 'tis better that men die with forgiveness in their hearts.

Only for a moment did Fidette stand gazing down into the upturned faces of these pitiless assassins. I feared that her courage had failed her; but I was mistaken.

Still clinging to the standing rigging with her left hand, she took with her right hand from the little wicker basket four of the pretty yellow bombs, and, true to the mark, sent them hurtling toward the deck.

They landed simultaneously and quite near together in the centre of the human square.

The concussion that instantly followed shook every timber of the ship. It could not be described as an explosion, but as a white flash. Very little flame was seen, but the deck was cleared as if by magic. Pieces of wood and parts of human bodies were sent screaming through the air. The very oakum between the deck planks was converted into impalpable dust. The bulwarks were torn away on the starboard side, and all the invaders who stood there were brushed into the sea as with a broom.

On the port side, owing to the fact that the force of the explosion had been spent in the opposite direction, a few men escaped. Many of these were wounded, and several were suffering from shock.

Fidette had recaptured the ship!

CHAPTER XIX.

FIDETTE BECOMES MINE.

Exactly six of the boarding party escaped. Trembling with fear inspired by the sudden and terrible death that had overtaken their companions on the deck of the Happy Shark, they sprang into the water and hid themselves under their floating spar.

"Out with the boats and follow them!" cried Fidette, her voice no longer gentle and sweet.

Unfortunately, all our boats had been destroyed, and no posible means of pursuit remained. I was just as glad, because our experience in the boats earlier in the day had not been calculated to inspire confidence in such an attack. What was left of the attacking party was sure to escape. In numbers they were few, but in resources and artifices they were strong. They deserved no mercy. They had made a wanton and heartless attack upon us, and had robbed us of our good commander. They had made Fidette an orphan.

When pursuit was seen to be impossible, I watched the infernal spar slowly moving out into the centre of the Grand Canal. Then I turned my attention to the dead and dying that strewed our decks. Many of the killed were frightfully mangled. The explosion of the shell having torn up the deck, the flying splinters killed as many men as did the concussion.

I gave immediate orders to have all the bodies of the invaders thrown over the side of the ship. This was done without any feeling of remorse.

We gathered our own dead, and I gave orders to have them prepared for burial.

Poor Fidette was inconsolable. I found her bending over the body of her father, wailing piteously!

Examining the old man's body, I found that he had died from a knife thrust in the heart. The scoundrel who had dealt the blow was a swarthy Lascar, and he had, fortunately for himself, died from the wound inflicted by the Kantoon. Had he still been alive, I am sure I could not have restrained our men from inflicting upon him the most horrible tortures. Remember, they would have felt little resentment toward him for the murder of the good Kantoon; what incensed them specially was the mutilation prior to the final extinction of the old man's life.

Reverently lifting the Kantoon's body in my arms, I carried it to his cabin and placed it in his bunk; then, with a deep feeling of sorrow in my heart, I withdrew, leaving poor Fidette alone with her dead father.

Obviously, the first thing to be done was to call a meeting of the entire ship's company.

This I did at once, and the men soon assembled in front of the mainmast. Speaking in the same polyglottic tongue that the good Kantoon had employed, I addressed the men in as pathetic a manner as I could, calling attention to the bravery of our dead commander, and then commending by name all the valorous sailors who lay dead.

I then approached the important subject of the succession to the Kantoonship. I desired to be the master of the Happy Shark, but I was well aware that the first and second mates had prior claims, and would not quietly relinquish them.

Under the Sargasson code, each Community is a law unto itself. If the crew wished to have me rule over them no influence could prevent me from attaining that dignity. Had I already been Fidette's husband, of course I would have become the commander without question.

Rebellion was rampant throughout the Sargasso Sea, and although there had not been any signs of mutiny aboard my own vessel, I felt that if I insisted upon becoming captain of the ship it would be fomented.   I decided to temporize for a few days, until I could be married to Fidette under the civil form, after which my claim would be well nigh unimpeachable.

I therefore concluded my address to the men by saying that pending any final decision regarding the Kantoonship, we would unite in a common sorrow, and attend the burial of our late commander.

The rebellious condition of the Sargassons made it dangerous for Fidette and me to undertake a journey to the Priest of the Sacred Fire. We might not have been molested, but the chances were that a marauding party or some friends of the men defeated upon our decks would give chase and destroy us.   Besides, the code of this people provided for civil marriages in the presence of witnesses during stress of heavy weather—not that the waves ever ran very high on the large canals of Sargasso, because the sea was held in bondage by the thick green blanket of weeds and orchids that thrived luxuriously upon its heaving surface.

A superstitious people, the Sargassons feared intensely the electric storms that broke over them.   Like the sailors of Columbus, they had a dread of falling stars. A yellow condition of the atmosphere completely prostrated them.   Mere rainstorms were to them a delight. It was the commonest incident to see the entire ship's company mustered to enjoy a heavy rain!   I had seen the Kantoon awaken his sturdiest men out of their first sleep at the end of a watch, in order that they might be brought on deck again and stand in a shower.

Not a moment was to be lost if I were to retain command of the ship.

At the side of the body of her dead father, Fidette and I calmly and solemnly discussed the situation.   She agreed with me entirely that our marriage must occur at once. In a girlish way, she exacted of me only one promise, and that was that I would never refer to the trombone man after our marriage. As her poor dead father had "arranged" the Portuguese's taking off, I saw no reason why I should ever dwell upon the man's existence. I promised.

We agreed, though not without serious controversy, that it was wisest to have the ceremony take place while her father's body still remained on the ship. It was to us a palladium of safety, for in its visible presence no vandal hand would dare to intrude and take possession of the Kantoon's cabin.

The civil ceremony of marriage among the Sargassons is simplicity itself. The bride and the groom approach the mainmast from opposite ends of the vessel, she always leaving her cabin in the stern of the boat, and he going forward, in order that, returning, he may approach from the bow. In the presence of the entire ship's company drawn up along the bulwarks, the contracting parties join both hands around the mainmast. They then move three times completely around the mast in order that every member of the ship's company shall witness the fact that they have voluntarily taken each other as husband and wife. They then unclasp their hands and standing facing each other aft the mast. After that, one of the crew, generally the oldest man, no matter what his station, presents the bride with a sprig of bay or other green bough. The groom then makes his bride a present of a necklace of shark's teeth and a few pink-fish scales, with pretty sentiments indelibly scratched upon them.

If the groom have the promise of the succession to the command of a vessel in Sargasso, it is usually good form to announce it on such an occasion. I had no such promise in writing, nor had Fidette, the fact being that I had hoped to be transferred to my old ship and resume command of her.

In the absence of the officiating Kantoon, it is the custom for the groom to ask the bride, in the presence of all the witnesses, if she willingly and freely accepts him to be her husband, and in the event of a favorable response, the bride then puts a similar question to her intended mate, which, if properly replied to, confirms the union, and all the sailors unite in a benediction in the words:

"It is well; amen."

With much solemnity the best friend of the groom approaches, carrying a bucket of water, ascends to a small platform that has been put up for the occasion, and while the newly wedded pair bow their heads in a respectful attitude, they receive The Baptism. Rain water is generally used upon occasions of this kind.

So we were married.

This being the conclusion of the ceremony, the bride always kisses her husband first, and he, throwing himself upon his face upon the deck, returns the salute by planting a kiss upon each of her pretty pink feet, in token of abject reverence.

Under ordinary circumstances, a period of feasting and dancing would have followed. But the dead body of the good Kantoon still lay unburied.

The Sargassons have a very pretty theory about death.

They believe that those to whom the messenger comes when the sun is shining brightly are transported straight away to the sweet-water heaven, where they may wade and disport themselves to all eternity. To those, on the other hand, who receive the call of death in the hours of darkness or in foggy weather, there must needs be a preparatory period before they can enjoy the future life. I never met a Sargasson who was not a believer in fore-ordination. What is to be they believe will be. While I witnessed many deathbed scenes, I never heard a reproach or a regret uttered that the end did not come

when most desirable. Those who passed away in the
night accepted the verdict as a punishment for some act,
known or unknown, committed by them during their
lives.

The funeral of the Kantoon took place on the following day. The dear old man was sewed up in the
only bit of tarpaulin left on board, and, weighted with our
last anchor, was brought to the gangway. There we all
took our final leave, after the Sargasson form, each member of the ship's company approaching solemnly, with
bared head, and placing his right hand over the heart
of the dead. No sound of lamentation or grief was expressed or permitted, but the body, resting on a long
board, was gently pushed, feet foremost, into the sea.

Half an hour later, while I was busied with my
duties in getting the ship in trim, little Fidette had taken
her place far out on the bowsprit, and sat dangling her
feet in the water, nursing her prettiest and most petted
pink and green octopus.

CHAPTER XX.

MAKING NEW BOATS.

Good fortune does not always bring happiness. This turn in my affairs, however, attractive from a Sargasson viewpoint, caused me heartache. The death of the good Kantoon had changed the whole current of my life. My marriage with Fidette, that I had counted upon to seal the promise of her father to have the command of my old ship at her moorings, not far distant, was the tie that now bound me absolutely to the Happy Shark. Without the potent influence of the dead commander, I could hardly hope, newcomer as I was, to be selected for the important trust I coveted.

The courage that I had shown during the attack of the boarding party had reconciled all the opposing factions to my leadership and command. If, indeed, I had lacked anything in spirit or ferocity, Fidette's unexampled success with the mock oranges confirmed me in my position.

I would be associated with the other Commanders in the Seaweed Sea; would assemble and kneel with them around the Sacred Fire at the annual Guna-Gamus.

Participation in this solemn ceremonial was proof of social recognition beyond all certificates of character.

And yet, I was not happy.

Deep down in my heart, I had harbored treachery to the Sargassons. One of my constant dreams had been to regain possession of the Caribas, that I might repair her machinery, store her with dried seaweed and other drift, with which to feed her boilers long enough to get up steam and reclaim the lost ship for her owners.,

My own release from the enforced detention did not excite my imagination nearly so much as the prospect of returning to the owners at Plymouth the property that they had intrusted to my care.

Torn by conflicting emotions of love and duty, I was the most miserable of men. I could not forget Fidette. Equally hard was it for me to overlook the countless kind acts that I had received from the Sargasson people. They had robbed me of my command; had dishonored me in my own eyes; but theirs was a novel piracy, so curious and interesting that I forgave the injustice to me.

Besides, there was much to be said in behalf of the Sargassons. Other nations, whose people are far more civilized, indulge in conquests, make war without due provocation, capture ships, burn towns and massacre innocent people. To the Sargassons, a constant accession of new ships and new blood is necessary. They are not a prolific people. From their point of view, any ship that strays or adventures within the limits of their domain is lawful prize. They make war upon no other part of the world! Their possessions are far out of the ordinary path of trade, and misfortune and foolishness are the only two excuses for an invasion of Sargasso. It is true, they are merciless and cruel. In their battles they neither give nor accept quarter; but such is the Draconian law they practice against each other.

It is perfectly natural that they should discountenance the escape of any adventurer who may have become possessed of the secret of their existence.

Every ship in Sargasso is a treasure house, loaded with the salvage of derelicts from every quarter of the habitable globe. No government to-day in existence, recognizes the rights of the Sargassons. The limits of their strangely organized republic are undefined. Like the Numancians of old, they perish by self-destruction rather than surrender to external foes. Sleeping or waking, each member of a ship's company exists only at the mercy of the Kantoon who commands the craft.

The bottom of every ship is a honeycomb of holes, the plugs in which can be drawn by means of chains leading to the Commander's cabin.

Therefore, I say, the fact that I have returned to my native land and am able to recount my curious experiences is solely due to the fact that the mercy and kindness of the Sargassons in my case were misplaced. For their own protection they should have made way with me. The recent account of the Bureau of Navigation at Washington, directing that several of the smaller armed cruisers be sent to the Sargasso Sea for the purpose of blowing up and sinking all the vessels found therein, is the result of an indiscreet communication made by me shortly after my return a few weeks ago.

I need not say that this is to me a matter of sincere regret, that our Government, having many humane acts to its credit, should thus ruthlessly intrude upon a people that has never personally harmed it, and wage a war of extermination not equaled even by the savage and uncivilized Sargassons.

Can it be that the United States is about to follow the example of Japan at Port Arthur!

In my behalf, it should be remembered that I was still in the honeymoon of love.

Life had never seemed so precious to me; and the thought that the Happy Shark could not be expected to keep afloat for many years filled me with mental agony. Here must we stay, exactly like rats on a sinking ship.

The thought of death grew more repugnant to me every day. I didn't want to lose Fidette.

The crew were set to work making new boats.

This was imperative for several reasons. First of all, we were very short of food on the Happy Shark. The sides of the vessel had been scraped clean of all barnacles—the small shellfish being very attractive to the Sargasson palate.

The quaking sod for miles around was covered with a luxuriant growth of yellow berries, delicious to the taste. Crayfish existed in great abundance. They climbed out of the water on the branches of floating trees, and could be gathered in large quantities. The fruit and the crayfish were eaten raw.

It was necessary, also, that we should have new boats, because the ceremony of the Guna-Gamus would soon occur, and my first appearance at that function must not be prevented.

The selection of the material from which the boats were made was a matter of considerable difficulty as well as art.

From the under surface of the floating sod long, ropelike roots extended downward to great depths. These roots were of a brownish hue and varied in thickness. They were very pliable while fresh, and were readily worked up into matting.

There was only one way in which this material could be procured. The thickness of the sod varied greatly, according to the period of its formation. It was necessary, therefore, to find a thin spot in the sod, through which a hole could be cut. Divers, armed with short, sharp knives, were sent down to bring these long, ell-like roots to the surface. This work was attended with much danger, because it not infrequently happened that the diver became confused while working under the sod, and, losing his bearings, groped his way in a direction opposite the watery shoot through which he had descended. Rescue was impossible.

Now and then a shark devoured a diver.

When enough of these roots had been secured by

this hazardous means, they were lashed together and kept in the water until the moment of their use.

A stout and straight limb was cut from one of the floating trees for a keel. The finding of this stick was not easy.

I should have mentioned that as soon as possible after the final defeat of the boarding party, who had attempted to capture and assassinate us, swimmers were s nt out, and succeeded in securing and dragging back to the ship several of our destroyed canoes.

The keel, generally nine feet in length, was placed upon a row of blocks, several inches above the deck. Five pieces of the longest and toughest roots were selected by the expert boatmaker, and these were placed around and parallel to the keel stick. They were then carefully bound together by the smallest and the toughest withes, made of roots split in half. This part of the work required much skill and neatness. The excellence of the completed boat depended upon the firmness with which these long, radiating roots were bound to the keel.

The long ends of two of the roots projecting from the keel were brought together about two feet above the blocks, and there securely fastened. They were then gently bent at right angles and extended in a curved line from stem to stern, and vice versa. This formed the gunwales of the boat. The other withes were then turned backward, and attached at regular intervals to the gunwale line. This formed a rough network, over which the smaller roots were laced with consummate art, until every crevice was covered.

Meanwhile, the gum made from fish scales was in preparation, and this was carefully smeared over the entire network within and without, rendering the boat absolutely water tight. The secret of the composition of this glue was one of the treasured possessions of the Sargassons.

When completed, the boats weighed usually about

thirty pounds. It was necessary that they be kept wet
all the time, however, as they became worthless when
once thoroughly dried.

A direct means existed for communicating with the
neighboring ships. In my excursions I had noticed
bundles of the cordlike roots radiating from various
ships across the floating sod—submerged at points, but
generally out of the water. They were similar to the
roots used by the Sargassons in the construction of their
boats. These roots extended downward to great lengths,
limited only by their tensile strength. I have seen many
specimens one thousand feet long. They drew their entire sustenance from the water, and a bit of root thrown
overboard would continue to live, and finally attach itself
to the sod.

The Sargassons formed long cables of these roots,
by grafting them together at the ends and covering the
splices' with fish scale gum. The wounds soon healed
and the junction became perfect. In this way the Sargassons pieced the roots together until they were many
miles in length. The cables thus formed were rarely
more than an inch in diameter, but they possessed the remarkable property of transmitting sound. This system of
intercommunication had been introduced by a Ceylonese,
who, proud of the traditions of his imperial island, had recalled to mind the grapevine telegraph that once joined
together the entire coast of his native land. Messages
were transmitted by blows upon a solid block of wood
attached to the end of the root cable. I never mastered
the code, but our signal officer, an old Frenchman, was
quite expert.

One of the most interesting episodes of hist ry was the
attempt of the Dutch to take possession of Ceylon. They already possessed Java and other islands of less size. in
Oceania, and in their stately ships they made a serious
attempt to capture the valuable island south of Hindus-
tan. But the Ceylonese were proud of their independ-

ence. Religious fanaticism also had much to do with their sturdy courage. Were they not the custodians of the sacred tooth of Buddha? The Western infidels, as they very naturally denominated the Hollanders, would not respect this trophy. Therefore, they of Ceylon must answer for it to Buddha with their lives.

Again and again the Dutch attempted to land troops, but they were always confronted with native soldiery, who beat them off, destroyed their boats, and massacred all the officers and men who escaped the savage surf that beat upon the Ceylon shores. In vain the would-be invaders resorted to artifice. They sailed away at night, as if abandoning the attack, only to approach the island at another point, but always to find the courageous and unconquerable natives drawn up in martial array to receive them. The attempt to capture the island was abandoned. It was claimed, quite in the Eastern fashion, that intercommunication was effected after the manner of the Theosophists, by the projection of thought. or by actual traveling of the astral body. This explanation satisfied the Hollanders. Subsequent exploration, after the island became a part of British India, made it plain that through the tree tops of Ceylon's trackless forests were carried grapvine cables, possessing the capacity of transmitting sound. By a system of telegraphy, known only to themselves, they could reproduce at a far distant end of such a vegetable cable the sounds made by sharp blows of a hammer. In this way they were able to transmit information and to indicate accurately the point at which, from the highest headland, the enemies' ship could be seen approaching.

Nothing could have better served the purpose of the Sargassons for the transmission of information than these long, woody-hearted roots. The absence of pith greatly increased the power of conducting sound. Although the vessel of the Chief Kantoon was a day's journey distant, it was possible to send a communication thither and receive an answer in about two hours.

The problem of reprovisioning the Happy Shark
became one of serious moment. Dissatisfaction was
spreading among the men, and my supremacy was seriously threatened.

During short journeys across a part of the floating
sod, I had noticed that the tree branches submerged in the
water were covered with small shell fish, like young
oysters. I had a large quantity of these bivalves collected, and deliberately flew in the face of the Sargasson
law that prohibited fire on the ships by having a chowder
prepared. There was a large boiler on the forward part
of the main deck of the Happy Shark, just over the fo'castle, and at night I set a fire going under it. I dared not
cook in the daytime, because the column of ascending
smoke would have indicated me as a violator of the laws.
The boatswain produced the flame in the most primitive
fashion by sharpening a stick at both ends and twirling
it by means of a silversmith's bow and cord until it ignited.

The odor of food was soon perceptible about the
ship. All the men were awakened and served with a
dish of the stew. I thickened it with pieces of sun-dried
farina, and flavored it with some of the herbs that I had
discovered growing wild upon the green meadows.

In a few days this new addition to the Sargasson cui-
sine made me the most popular commander in all the
community.

But one doesn't have to go to the Seaweed Sea to
learn that if you touch a man's stomach you win his
heart.

CHAPTER XXI.

I BECOME A SARGASSON.

Soon after the events narrated in the previous chapter I was busy at noonday taking an observation as to our exact latitude and longitude, when Fidette came running to me with the astonishing announcement that a large galley was coming down the Grand Canal, making straight for the Happy Shark. I laid down my quadrant and called all the men to quarters. I had no means of knowing whether the call was a friendly or unfriendly one. Our boats were not entirely completed, and, had they been, we could not have offered any real resistance to this large war canoe with its thirty men.

The first mate was sent forward to speak the craft as soon as she came within hailing distance, and he returned with the information that the men in command of the boat bore a communication from the High Priest of the Sacred Fire. We were summoned, Fidette and I, to the august presence, in order that the religio⁻s marriage ceremonies might be performed.

Here was a perilous situation for me.

Nearly three days would be required for the complete journey, during which I had no guarantee that my men would not overthrow my supremacy. I likewise doubted the good faith of the High Priest, and of the barbarians he had sent to conduct us to him. When, however, the formidable document was passed over the ship's side and Fidette had carefully scrutinized the writing upon the tarpon scales, she decided that we dare not disregard the command.

The thought promptly suggested itself to me that the crew of the Unk-ta-hee, as the Priest's barge was called, should be invited on board and fed. I was about to give an order to that effect, when, fortunately, I consulted the first mate, and learned that such a custom is entirely unheard of in Sargasso—the distrust being so general that no Kantoon would seriously contemplate inviting more than two or three strange men on board his ship at one time. I then saw that the visiting boat had come fully provisioned, for the men began to eat their midday meal while they rested.

Naturally, Fidette desired to present herself in as attractive a manner as possible before the Archimandrite of the floating monastery. This strange and mysterious place was an object of dread to most of the inhabitants of the archipelagic community. It was never visited by any citizen of Sargasso, except on just such occasions as this, and the strictest secrecy was always enjoined upon those who had been there.

In less than an hour after the formal command of the High Priest had been delivered to us. I had placed my ship in charge of the first mate, and, taking with me only a few articles of wearing apparel and my chronometer and quadrant (which I had never allowed to go out of my possession for an instant since their return to me), I awaited Fidette outside her cabin, prepared to make the voyage on the Unk-ta-hee.

This boat was about sixty feet long, fashioned from a solid tree trunk, and resembled an African war canoe.

The dear little woman lingered over her toilet. She knew the hardships of the journey, and brought with her some sea-grass blankets. Finally she appeared, and, tripping across the deck of the Happy Shark toward me, she waved an adieu to all her old shipmates. The spectacle affected me very deeply. These grizzly men, most of

whom had known Fidette from her earliest infancy, were
affected to boisterous laughter—that being the Sargasson
method of expressing sorrow.

Tears were unknown among the People of the Salted
Seas.

As we crossed the side of the ship to enter the Unk-
ta-hee, we observed that a small but neat cabin had been
fitted up astern for my Fidette. It was a rude affair, formed
of reed matting, and occupied a space in the barge just
aft the chief paddler. It was barely long enough for
the little creature to rest at full length, but was without
a roof to protect the inmate from the rain or dew.
As I have said before, Sargassons never desired to be
sheltered from the rain; had they dwelt in houses, like
other people, their structures would have been roofless.
The heat of the sun was very oppressive to them. Had
the crew of the Happy Shark lived ashore they probably
would have burrowed in the ground and passed the heat
of the day in cellars.

No sooner had Fidette and I stepped into the great
barge than the command was given to push off, and after
a few moments the paddlers gradually increased the speed
of the heavy wooden canoe.

We stood up in the open part of the barge, waving
a farewell to our comrades on the Happy Shark. We did
not know that we were taking final leave of the vessel.
As long as possible we kept the dear old craft in sight.
To Fidette the tenderest memories centred about the
only home she had ever known.

We were bound upon a journey, the exact purport
of which we did not understand, and we were troubled in
our minds as to its outcome.

On the barge, which sat low in the water, it was not
possible to keep the Happy Shark in sight for more than
an hour. At the end of that time new scenes and new incidents attracted our attention, and the long afternoon
passed agreeably. We were rowed within close prox-

imity to more than two hundred derelicts, all inhabited, all having their individual social organizations, and all amenable to the supreme direction of the Chief Kantoon, who existed on some far-away and stately ship, unseen and unknown by sight to almost everybody in the entire nation, but always revered, respected and obeyed.

Just at dark we passed very near a ship in the last stages of dry rot. The antique craft had become so excessively buoyant that it stood high out of water, and was liable to capsize at any moment. The crew of that vessel might have allowed some water to enter the hold to have submerged their craft to the load line, but they dared not remove the plugs from the hull, for when these were once extracted by the Kantoon, with the ceremonial usual on such occasions, Sargasson formality forbade a stopping of the inflow of water.

To me the scene was very pathetic, and I imagined that I could see in the resigned and beatific countenances of the various members of the crew a foreknowledge of their impending doom. I nowhere saw any exhibitions of fear, desire to escape, or, what was equally sad to me, of hope.

As we progressed, the ships were arranged more closely together—less intervening sod separating them.

The twilight was very brief, but just before the sun took its last drop into the water and night came, we passed a vessel on which was a band of musicians, who produced the most extraordinary noises that had ever greeted my ears. The instruments were chiefly of wood, constructed after the manner of dulcimers, and the musical sounds were produced by beating upon strips of wood of various sizes, which hung from the standing rigging. The effect was weird, and, although a defective note frequently marred the harmony, it was a pleasing diversion, not only for the Sargassons, but for me. Our thirty paddlers were allowed to rest and listen to the Sargasson national hymn.

The commander of the barge took advantage of the opportunity, and served supper to all hands.

One of the darkest nights I ever experienced in my whole career at sea followed. The moon was at the full, but a mass of clouds, black as ink, obscured her and the evening star.

We soon composed ourselves to sleep. The sturdy men at the paddles evidently slept while they worked. No galley slaves toiled more unceasingly than did this volunteer crew of Sargassons, intent only on my formal admission to all the sacred rights of this strange people.

A perfect knowledge of the route over which we traveled was shown by the commander. He steered the craft with a large oar, which he shifted from one side to the other, as was necessary, on occasions exerting great strength where a sharp turn was to be made. Not a light was in sight.

Even my practiced eyes could not distinguish the &nd line that formed the banks of the canal, and I fully appreciated the difficulty of the pilot's work.

As dawn came, we were awakened by the singing of birds. We rose and looked about us. The men were still laboring at the paddles with swaying bodies, all moving in unison, their heads resting on their arms, and their faces, with tightly closed eyes, turned from the glare of the rising sun. The air was very balmy, and the sky was as blue as it is in Andalusia in early Spring.

Fidette and I stood up and gazed upon the scene. Larks and mocking birds could be heard on all sides, singing cheerily. Only a short distance ahead we beheld the open water of the Inland Sea, at the further side of which we had been informed was moored the floating palace of the Chief Kantoon. I had no trouble in getting my bearings. The rising sun clearly indicated the east, and on consulting the small compass that I always carried, I found that the needle had suddenly swung four points from due north, and now pointed directly to the northwest. Some new magic influence had evidently affected the needle! I recalled the fact that Columbus, in his journeys, had experienced a somewhat similar deviation in the mid-Atlantic, although he only skirted the outer edge of the Sargasson continent.

The silence of this vast Inland Sea was depressing. Although we were in the mid-Atlantic, the far-stretching blanket of sod that lay upon the bosom of the deep, repressed its energy to such a degree that the ordinary swell of the ocean was barely noticeable. Literally, it was a tideless sea. I had expected that the Sargassons would paddle boldly out into the centre of this large lake, but the commander carefully kept near the sod bank that outlined it.

It was high noon when we approached the huge ark where dwelt the Chief Kantoon. We were expected, and the gangway of the ship was neatly trimmed with sea grass matting of brilliant hues.

We soon rowed alongside, and, with some trepidation, I took Fidette's hand and assisted her up the steps. We were received on deck by a young priest in full vestments, while a choir of boys sang what was evidently a hymn of welcome. Not a word of reception was spoken. After bowing low, we were immediately taken to a cabin, in the centre of which was a table laden with fruit, and upon which, to my amazement, stood a flagon of orange-hued wine, evidently of native manufacture. I had not had the opportunity to dampen my palate with anything of the kind for so many months that, when an attendant poured me out a cup of the pale yellow fluid, I accepted it and drank without hesitation. Fidette did the same.

During this entertainment, I had an oportunity to look around the cabin. It was the most curious wonder-shop I had ever entered. Its walls were hung with shields and pieces of silverware. Hundreds of quaint knives and cutlasses were assembled in clusters on the ceiling and in the corners. Trophies from every ship that had joined the community were to be seen. Priceless gems, in antique settings, were arranged in rosettes upon the grass-cloth draperies. Beautiful articles of beaten gold, evidently fashioned from nuggets, formed by melting down that most useless commodity among the Sargassons, the coin of commerce, rested upon the table and upon the shelves in various parts of the cabin.

Indeed, we ate our modest luncheon of berries and oranges from golden dishes.

CHAPTER XXII.

A SOLEMN CEREMONIAL.

In excellent French the attendant instructed us as to our part in the approaching ceremonial. Two robes of Chinese silk, reaching to our feet, were handed us, and we were told to array ourselves. I was very glad of this, as I had only partially adopted the garb of the Sargassons, and my clothing was badly worn and shiny. Fidette, I imagine, was much annoyed at this suggestion, not wishing to make the change from the pretty costume of grass-cloth that she had fashioned with her own fingers to the shroud-like garment, which did not set off her pretty figure to advantage. The orders of the attendant, however, were imperative, and we were soon ready for the solemn ceremonial.

When we were ready to meet the Chief Kantoon, we were attended by the same priest who had welcomed us to the ship, and we were also accompanied by the choir of boys, who, during our slow and solemn walk from the reception cabin to the large and imposing after-cabin, chanted a processional hymn.

Fidette appeared to be in an ecstasy of delight, but for my part I could not shake off the feeling that we were the central figures in a requiem mass, instead of a glorious ceremonial of sanctification. I was depressed, therefore, rather than exhilarated.

The after part of the ship, that had been prepared

for the initiation, was separated from the rest of the deck
by a hedge of orchids, growing in a series of rude boxes.
A doorway in the centre was covered by portieres of
grass-cloth, which, as we approached, were slowly drawn
apart.

As we entered, I was impressed with the beauty and
solemnity of the scene.

The Chief Kantoon sat upon a raised dais, directly
at the stern of the vessel, and on his immediate right,
equally elevated, sat the High Priest of the Sacred Fire.
He was vested in a chasuble of black, much after the
manner of the priests who celebrate mass in our American churches. Near him and behind were ranged attending acolytes, wearing long copes of lustreless, sea-green
hue. To the immediate left of the Chief Kantoon stood
the six members of his cabinet. They were all savage-
visaged men, dressed in simple tunics, woven of sea
grass, and bare as to their arms and legs. Without any
of the sacred character that appertained to the priesthood
near by, they possessed a far more imposing aspect.
Their complexions were all sun-bronzed. Their figures
recalled pictures that I had seen in books of the Huns
that overran the Roman Empire.

While I was making these observations, a double
line of Seminarians had ascended from the lower deck;
separating at the mainmast, one column had passed to
the right and one to the left, completely encircling us as
we stood in the centre of the sky-roofed cabin. Without
any prelude or observable signal, the attending priests
and Seminarians broke forth in a Kyrie-like invocation,
quite resembling the first movement of the mass in the
Roman churches immediately preceding the communion
service. This was of brief duration, and at its conclusion
the High Priest of the Sacred Fire, who had remained
standing throughout the Kyrie, took up the solemn ceremonial of the Water Worshipers. Speaking chiefly in
Portuguese, but following the usage of the Sargassons

and interpolating words of French, English, Italian, German and Spanish wherever his vocabulary failed him, the High Priest offered a rhapsody to the sea, which I venture to translate in the following language:
"The Ocean. It covereth all. It telleth nothing. It is silent—secretive as the dead ones. Death is our portion. It endeth all. It maketh us glad. We are of the sea, for it encompasseth us about like a mantle, shielding us from the miseries of the savage world."

Here the choir broke forth into a Kyrie Eleison, in words that might be interpreted:
"O most gracious Ruler of the Seaweed Sea, be merciful unto us. Amen."

Following which the High Priest of the Sacred Fire continued:
"Hail, welcoming arms of the Sea! We are at peace upon thy heaving bosom. Thy warm breath enchants us. We are as driftwood in thy grasp. Do thou, O glorious Sea, continue to endure us. We love thee. No other thoughts but of thee constrain us. Do suffer us to exist, that we may know thou ever loveth us."

As the High Priest paused, the choir again chanted:
"Adoration ever. O forgiving Sea, endure us."

Resuming, the High Priest said: "Hail to the attendants of the Sea, the Clouds—the homeless, wandering Clouds. Like unto us are they. Nor home, nor friends; but, like us, are they of the elements of the sea and not of the land. 'Tis ours to roll and roll till life doth cease to be. O splendid, boundless Sea, the wealth of all the world is thine; and with thee the burning sun, the cold, pale moon and the twinkling stars make merry company. Thou art eternal. None may measure thee or sound thy depths. Amen."

At a signal from an attending acolyte, Fidette and I knelt, slightly turning our bodies so that we directly faced the Chief Kantoon, who, raising high a glowing marlinspike heated to whiteness in the Sacred Fire, administered the following oath:

"By the hope of enduring mercy from the Grand
Kantoon who suffereth us not to sink, by the potency of
the Sacred Fire that burneth for ages and is not consumed, we take this oath of homage to the Ocean and
fidelity to the Sea, and here accept the people of Sargasso.
Thou, O Sea, shalt we honor and serve all the days of
our life; thou shalt we uphold and defend—live for and
die for. And in evidence of the sacred character of this
oath, here, in the presence of the High Priest of the
Sacred Fire that burneth forever and is not consumed,
do we declare our lives forfeit if in thought or act we
shall be wanting in fidelity to the People of the Sea. And
we appoint as our executioners any living, breathing
creature of the Sea or Air if treason be fastened upon us.
We devoutly appeal to the Grand Kantoon of the Sea
and Land, Keeper of the Homeless Clouds, to strengthen
us in this faith."

We having made satisfactory responses, the Chief
Kantoon stepped forward and touched each of us on the
bared right shoulder with the glowing marlinspike.

As we rose to our feet, the attending choir again
broke out into the joyous anthem of the Water Worshipers.

"Blessed be the name of the Sea.

"Majestic is the Ocean by day; sole.nn by night.

"Ours is the Sea and Sky. They are boundless.
None shall intrude upon us."

The High Priest then raised his hands and pronounced the benediction. Immediately the Chief Kantoon stepped down from the throne, and, holding out a
hand to each of us, graciously suffered it to be kissed.
Then, drawing from his girdle a sheaf of inscribed tarpon
scales, he selected two, of which he handed me the first,
saying:

"I herewith confer upon you the title of Kantoon in
token of your union with our people." Then, tendering
me the second scale, with its pale blue inscription, he

concluded: "You are restored to your ship, and from this moment are the commander of the Caribas. He who is at present in charge will, upon the presentation of this token, destroy himself after an old and accepted belief among the Sargassons that when a Kantoon is superseded he must disappear forever. Retrogression is disgrace! This commander whom you supplant has been treacherous to others, and it is our fear that he will be treacherous to us. Therefore give I you this ship. It is yours. Possess it, if necessary, at the point of the knife."

The announcement that we were not to return to the Happy Shark filled poor Fidette with anguish. She burst into a flood of tears that no words from me could check. I couldi not blame her. Her entire life was identified with her old home, but she was too familiar with the laws of her people not to know that no wish of hers would have any influence upon the Chief Kantoon.

To me the change from the Happy Shark to the Caribas was welcome. I felt that I would be more contented. I knew that the stanch iron vessel would remain afloat at least thirty years, and I was satisfied to accept that span of life. By that time, thought I, our love may have grown cold, and both Fidette and I may welcome the end.

I was now a Sargasson by all the sacred laws, and, had I had the entire fleet of vessels to choose from, I certainly would have selected my own ship, to which I had been so graciously assigned.

I was bewildered by the incidents that followed. We were surrounded by all the dignitaries of the Sargasson people. We were conducted to the table and invited to partake of the fruits and shellfish there bestowed. We were exhilarated and refreshed with copious libations of the orange-hued wine before mentioned.

Then succeeded merrymaking and a dance combining the most hilarious features of the Bamboola, Cachucha, Tarantella, Money Musk and Virginia Reel. It was, if anything, more violent than the famous "Dance of the Derelicts," which always closed the "Week of Silence." This I have previously described. In the sports, Fidette won great praise.

The daughters of the other Kantoons in the community, to the number of forty, were present, but none of them looked so pretty or behaved so charmingly as my own Fidette.

I accepted my fate.

One can be miserable in other places than Sargasso. I know something of the "civilized" world. In it are toil and sorrow—yes, worry and want. All the misery in New York is not found in the slums. It exists elsewhere. With my own eyes have I seen men stalking about the streets and exchanges suffering the mental tortures of the damned.

We call that civilization.

CHAPTER XXIII.

THE NEW LIFE.

The hour for our departure to our new home approached. Twilight, that period of indefinite length between darkness and daylight, was at hand. The sun had disappeared behind the western horizon for quite a time, and out a low cloudbank to the eastward, pale and cold as the Sargasson blood, rose the full moon, at first sight of which all the ship's company cast themselves upon their knees and worshiped. For the sun the Sargassons felt no respect. They saw it rise and set without emotion. To them "Apollo and his fiery steeds" never drove across the sky; to them no regnant orb of fire ruled supreme the brotherhood of worlds. To them the moon, so pale, so cold, so self-possessed, was Mistress of the Universe.

Our departure was invested with even more solemnity than our reception. We were reconducted to the cabin at the bow of the ship, where we resumed our clothing. In place of the short jacket that I had worn I received, as a gift, a coat of sun-tanned walrus skin that incased my burly form without a wrinkle.

The barge, with all its men in place, was awaiting us at the ship's side. I noticed at once that the paddlers were heavily armed. We descended, and were soon moving off along the shores of the tideless lake.

Before we had gone far, I observed that we were treated more deferentially than we had been on our upward journey. Nothing could have exceeded the respect shown us by the commander of the barge.

The effect of the pale moonlight upon the almost black surface of the Inland Sea was very striking. It made a path across the water as broad as a city thoroughfare, and, at the suggestion of Fidette, the man at the tiller kept our galley directly in this path of silver sheen. Our course lay eastward, and it was not until after midnight that we reached the outlet of the great lake. Although the coast line of floating sod was without any lighthouse or other marks of direction, the man who was directing the galley found no difficulty in entering the Grand Canal.

After the strange and curious events of the day, it was not remarkable that sleep should refuse to visit us.

Fidette and I were both suffering from the ghastly brand upon our shoulders, despite the attention which the surgeon on the ship of the Chief Kantoon had given us.

After midnight I fell into a troubled sleep, and did not awaken until broad daylight. Apparently, there was a strong current in our favor, because the oarsmen made very much better time returning than upon the upward journey. Although the Caribas was not in sight, I was able to recognize several landmarks.

A cold breakfast was served, consisting of baked shellfish and fruit, and we ate heartily. The men at the paddles had been fed about daylight, and had eaten as they worked.

The forenoon passed slowly. The sun was very warm, but the men never flagged in their steady and energetic stroke.

About 12 o'clock, as nearly as I could estimate, turning a sharp bend in the canal, the Caribas was descried straight ahead, distant about eight miles. I knew her instantly because of the excellent condition of her standing rigging. She was hull down, but I could not be mistaken about her topmast. I pointed out our future home to Fidette, and, as I expected, she indulged in a very womanish bit of crying. It was in vain that I attempted to divert her thoughts and told her of all the future happiness in store for her in our new home. I called her attention to the fact that all the joys that had been hers on the Happy Shark were gone. I dwelt upon the fact that it had been her father's wish that I should regain my ship. I spoke of its luxuries, its modern appliances, and in every way attempted to interest the dear little woman.

As we neared the Caribas, I detected our helmsman giving orders by signs, interjected with an occasional word that I did not understand. Although I called Fidette's attention to the circumstance, she was quite as unable to comprehend the meaning of the helmsman's conduct. Observing for myself, I saw that every man in the boat took out from its sheath and carefully examined a long, ugly-looking knife.

I feared that we were about to be assassinated.

With as much dignity as possible, I made my way to the stern of the boat and demanded an explanation of the officer.

He explained that he had special orders from the Chief Kantoon to place me in possession of my ship, and that he intended to do so. He expected opposition. The present captain of the Caribas was a plucky young man, who would fight. The contest would be apparently an uneven one, because the prize crew of the Caribas outnumbered the force in the galley two to one. He relied, however, upon the authority that was conferred upon him by the Chief Kantoon and the general respect for the ruler of the Sargassons. He believed that after he had publicly exhibited to the men on the Caribas the green tarpon scale, which would be recognized at once as a message from the Chief Kantoon, opposition would cease. The mutinous commander would be seized and promptly executed.

I felt regret at this summary disposal of my unknown rival. During the whole journey I had been attempting to conceive of some means by which his life might be spared. I hated to rise to power and influence over the dead body of a man who, I assumed, had never done me wrong, but I had not found any means of preventing the catastrophe. The will of the Chief Kantoon was law in Sargasso. Nobody, high or low, dared oppose it.

We were now within a cable's length of my old ship. In prospect of the change of commanders, the hull had been scraped of barnacles, and the dear craft looked as neat as in her palmiest days. Excepting the man on the bridge, I saw no evidence of life on the ship.

We reached the landing stage, that had been erected for the occasion, and the young officer in charge of our boat's crew fearlessly seized a dangling rope's end and climbed over the ship's side. He held in his teeth the talismanic tarpon scale. He knew, as I did, that it was his sole palladium of safety. Without it he would have been set upon the instant he touched the deck and cut to pieces. Close behind him followed twenty of the barge's crew. There was no concealment of the knives. After the crew, we slowly ascended amid the cheers of the ten men still remaining in the barge. Before emerging over the top of the bulwarks I had listened attentively for the clashing of arms; but I heard nothing, and, when I reached the deck, I saw nothing. Four stalwart members of our boat's crew stood there as guards, with the flesh-quivering knives in their hands.

In the after-cabin sat the late commander of the Caribas, tied in a chair, and as we were slowly conducted back, he turned his face in my direction.

To my surprise, I recognized the cause of all my trouble, Arthur Gray!

CHAPTER XXIV.

THE LAST OF AN ENEMY.

It was no time to gloat over the downfall of an enemy.

I had attained the coveted position of a Kantoonship among the Sargassons, and I was to occupy it at the expense of the life of the man who had been the means of bringing me among these strange people, who had just shown their appreciation and respect by conferring a high dignity upon me.

Unacquainted as I was with the history of Arthur Gray prior to my arrival in the community I could not pass judgment upon the acts of my fellow Sargassons. I had lost sight of Gray in the stirring events that had filled the previous months of my stay on the Happy Shark, and although it was considered quite improper to inquire regarding the fate of missing members of the community, I had tried, on several occasions, to ascertain what had become of him. I had been told that he was killed in the attack on the Caribas. There certainly had been some mystery attending the period of Gray's existence between that memorable capture and the fatal hour in which I again crossed his path. It was strange that we individually were responsible for the misfortunes that had overtaken each of us.

These thoughts were dominant in my mind as I

stood on the deck of my old ship, contemplating my now
humiliated and condemned enemy.   To his credit, I must
say that Gray did not evince any humiliation or seek to
curry favor.   He was already tightly bound in a peculiarly constructed chair, in which condemned Kantoons
were drowned.

This seat was made of three boards, fashioned quite
like a rustic chair found in our American Summer houses
and parks.   Into the longest piece of board was mortised
a seat, and this rude chair was made to stand by being
inclined backward and supported by a prop, similar to
that which holds an easel in position.   Devices like this
existed on every Kantoonment, in order that they might
be ready whenever wanted.

The custom under which each commander kept a
device for his own destruction in case of condemnation
may appear strange to those who are not familiar with
the habits of this people.   And yet, when a boy in the
United States, I remember distinctly to have known a
neighbor family that had resided for several generations
in the same dwelling-house.   With the boys of my own
age in this family I was on friendly terms, and I recollect
repeatedly to have been shown a broad board that was
carefully placed above the kitchen cupboard, and upon
which, I was gravely informed, all members of the Baxter
household were laid out and prepared for the grave.
That broad board was as much a part of the famliy possessions as its silverware, its cameo pins and other heirlooms.   I remember an occasion, when most of the members of the family were absent, the eldest boy and myself
carefully took the board from the cupboard, and, with
the assistance of two barrels, constructed a rude counter,
across which we dispensed vinegar soda water, grapevine-
leaf cigars and apples of suspicious character.

This was not in Sargasso, but in the suburbs of my
native city of Brooklyn.

"This must gratify you very much, Clark," began

Gray, in thoroughly good English. "I understand perfectly what hopes are awakened in your mind by your return to this ship, but I want to tell you that they are vain. You never can effect your escape from the Sargasso Sea!"

He was a mind-reader!

"What has become of the Secor launch?" I asked, tacitly confessing to the insinuation against me.

Gray's face assumed instantly an expression of contempt, as he sneeringly rejoined:

"I tried to escape in her, but in the absence of oil, I found it impossible. In my rage and chagrin I scuttled her. She is at the bottom of the sea."

The commander of the barge on which Fidette and I had reached our new home had been standing by during this conversation. Its acrimony was clearly observable, and when the first lull occurred in the conversation at this point, he touched Gray on the shoulder and said:

"Basta! You stoppa too longa." Then, turning to the half dozen sturdy fellows who stood beside him, he made a motion of his hand in the direction of Gray, and said in fairly good Spanish:

"Let him walk with God!"

The six executioners seized hold of Gray, carried him to the side of the ship, and, without any more ado, flung chair and occupant into the ocean.

As far as I could observe, nobody even looked over the side of the ship to see that poor Arthur Gray promptly sank beneath the brine.

The commander of the barge, acting as temporary executive of the Caribas, called all the men to quarters, and holding aloft in his right hand the same tarpon scales that had been handed to me by the Chief Kantoon, in the jargon of the Sargassons, officially proclaimed my elevation to the Kantoonship. At a signal from him, every man on board saluted, and the first mate, stepping forward, dropped to the right knee and bowed his head.

As I had been instructed to do, I touched him twice upon the right shoulder with a marlinspike and bade him arise. I assured him that he would still retain his post as executive of the Caribas. It was entirely within my power, by degrading him, to have condemned him to death. Had I seen fit to do so, or had any grudge provoked such an act, the first mate would have been instantly bound and tossed into the water, to share the fate of ex-Kantoon Gray.

My purpose in confirming the position of the first mate was that I might attach the crew to me in my new and trying position.

After partaking of a dinner that had been prepared for the crew of the barge on the main deck, its commander walked rapidly to the side of the ship, where was the ladder leading down to his boat. Without any formal farewell, he and his sturdy fellows resumed their places in the great canoe, and in a few minutes they were far out in the Grand Canal, bound homeward on their long journey, ending with their voyage across the tideless lake.

I then took formal possession of the ship.

I was surprised how few changes had been made in my cabin since that eventful morning when I had been induced to leave my ship and crew. In the centre of the deck, just below the cabin door, was a large blood stain, that marked the place of some brave fellow's death on the memorable night of the capture of the Caribas. Sturdy efforts had been made to efface this spot, but they had been unsuccessful. I found all my toilet articles just as I had left them; my brushes, combs and razors, and even a small bottle of brandy that had rested over my shaving stand, were undisturbed.

I have already spoken of the strict integrity and truthfulness of the Sargassons. Pilfering they held to be a crime so contemptible that only the basest savages indulged in it. Lying and stealing they classified together. Murder was not appalling to them, but during my stay in Sargasso I never knew or heard of a single case of treacherous assassination. Nobody was ever stabbed in the back or pushed into a shark's tank unexpectedly.

Fidette soon made herself very comfortable in the little cabin that adjoined mine, and showed signs of being reconciled to her separation from the Happy Shark.

CHAPTER XXV.

THE DANGER OF AN IDEA.

I had not been in command of the Caribas more than a month before I discovered that Donna Elenora, the wife of the Kantoon of the near-by ship Cormorant, and Fidette had their heads together and were engaged in the promulgation of a great socal reform. They were also in communication with other ships in our immediate neighborhood.

They had undertaken the laudable task of "ameliorating the condition of woman"—among the Sargassons.

I was prepared to admit that the status of woman among the Sargassons was not what it ought to be. She had considerable liberty, although she was not pampered with Parisian dresses and hats. She had no really laborious duties to perform, and, had she been inclined, might have devoted considerable time to the development of her mind and the beautifying of her person. I never had observed that she took advantage of her opportunities. Instead, therefore, of frowning upon the movement, I determined to encourage it by every means in my power.

No better field on the face of the sea or land could be found in which to give the woman question a supreme test.

I was a believer in woman's rights. I remembered the injustices under which my poor mother had suffered in South Brooklyn, and I was determined that if Fidette were bereft of any privileges she ought to have, I would see that they were conceded to her. All I wanted to know was whether the women of Sargasso could agree upon any policy that was reasonably sure to better their condition.

At the outset what threatened to be an insuperable barrier arose. The Sargassons have not a written language. Had they possessed a common tongue, it is doubtful if many of the women addressed could have deciphered the petitions. The brief verses or inscriptions written upon the tarpon scales, and that passed current for their literature, were chiefly extracts from the Spanish or Portuguese poets, badly memorized.

When the Sargasson women had once tasted the sweets of liberty, there was little doubt that they would improve intellectually, morally and physically. I remembered to have heard and read during my last shore life, heated arguments upon this very thing. I recalled the fact that a stubborn effort had been made to eliminate the word "male" from the constitution of my native State. I knew from my mother that, when she first entered the married state, she had no position recognized before the law. She had no legal right to her earnings; no legal right to direct and care for her children, and in politics she was absolutely denied any consideration whatever. I had often admitted in my own heart that a woman's life under such circumstances was necessarily unhappy, and I felt glad, owing to the active agitation of a few noble-hearted women, that most of the barriers restricting woman's progress and intelligence had been swept away. I was just as pleased that this was true as any woman could have been.

I recognized the fact also that woman had become a great industrial factor in the progress of the western world. She owned vast amounts of property, on which she was taxed, and, therefore, had a right to say what special uses she would prefer made of the money so exacted. Woman suffrage had been tried in one of our largest States, Wyoming, with good effect, and had there been found to improve home life instead of destroying it. I was a convert.

Sending for Fidette, I had a calm and very agreeable conversation with her upon the subject. She owned up, frankly, that she and Donna Elenora had undertaken to preach a propaganda against the subjective condition of woman in Sargasso. They believed that her superior intelligence and good looks entitled her to more consideration than she received. Fidette denounced the theory that among a people where women were few they received greater respect than in countries where they were many. She asserted what I recognized as a startling truth, that the great bulk of the personal property at present existing in Sargasso was in the hands of her sex.

As diamonds, pearls and other precious stones had no commercial value among the Sargasson people, it had been the custom, whenever a derelict was added to the group, to divide the jewels and silverware among the wives of the Kantoons. These in turn had passed the trinkets down to their daughters, and in that way many of the Sargasson women possessed jewel boxes that would have caused the noblest women of Europe to turn green with envy. Such a thing as a theft of jewels was unknown, because they never could be worn in public by the unlawful possessor, and, of course, escape to any part of the world where a market could be found was guarded against.

I entered heartily into the movement for bettering the condition of the Sargasson women.

Fidette was delighted. She foresaw the immortality that awaited her. Her name would be handed down through generations as the champion of her sex! In her ecstasy, she went to her cabin, took down her mandolin, and, in the quaint jargon of the Sargassons, sang, in words as light as air:

Wurra, wurra, wink-o-chee,
"Vous etes mucho fond o' me?"
No can marry esta girl
Quando jeune, y dans le whirl;
Mais, oui? Mais, non!
Pero—Hope on!

This jargon may be very freely translated thus:

Alack! alas! my own sea loon,
"For love of me you're in the moon?"
But you can't marry this one girl
While she's young and in the whirl,
You can? You can't!
But hope—hope on!

While Fidette sang I made merry with my memory. When I lived in Brooklyn I had a cousin who belonged to a wealthy family and was a member of a very famous woman's club called the Amazons, and from her I learned that after the ladies who belonged to that organization had possessed themselves of all the "rights" that could not make their escape, they began to wrangle with each other as to which of them should enjoy the acquired privileges. The idea of having them in common did not satisfy. One incident that I remember to have heard mentioned impressed me greatly. It arose out of the annual election for the presidency. The tall and stately dame who held that honored post very nearly failed of a renomination. There was considerable feeling in the club in opposition to her, but when she realized that a younger candidate was to be named in her stead she burst into a flood of tears and made a pathetic appeal to the assembly for a continuance in authority. The result was that the meeting closed with a semi-hysterical burst of tears on all sides.

The moral of this bit of retrospection is that I felt perfectly sure Fidette and Donna Elenora would be less confidential toward each other at the end of a month than they were at the moment of arranging their friendly compact. Therefore, not approving of the sociability that had sprung up between them, I believed that the quickest way to destroy it was to encourage it.

CHAPTER XXVI.

THE NEW WOMAN IN SARGASSO.

The captain's gig, which I had found in an excellent
state of preservation on one of the lower decks, was put
in the hands of one of the crew, who had some experience
as a carpenter, and was thoroughly refitted. I had the
seats in the stern of the boat covered with sea-grass
cushions and the trim gig given a coat of the fish-scale
shellac, without and within. There were seats for six
oarsmen.

When the gig was finished and the oars fitted thereto,
I selected a boat's crew with great care, choosing only
the strongest and homeliest young men from the ship's
company. When all was ready I had the boat placed in
the water one day when Donna Elenor was present on
the Carabas, and then informed the two ladies that the
gig was at their service, individually and collectively,
whenever they chose to use it. I knew enough of human
nature to foresee that, after a few visits together, the two
ladies would disagree as to the proper hour to make
calls, and practically would never use the boat in each
other's company. I must admit that I felt an emotion of
satanic delight in destroying all the traditions of the Sargassons at one blow, and in thus boldly introducing
what we in the English language denominate "The Sociability of the Human Race." Deep down in my heart I
felt that the Sargassons were right in theory and in practice.

Little as they knew of the great world that surrounded them, but of which they formed a part, they had
discovered that, almost universally, friendships exist because of mutual interests, and that the moment a prepon-
derance of selfish benefit accrues to one individual in
excess of that attainable by the other, all cordiality is
dissipated.

Friendship is a mirage of Fogland! It vanishes
when the sunlight of self-interest beats upon it.

In every way I encouraged the propaganda that
these good ladies had set on foot. Day by day I saw
them depart, filled with the enthusiasm of their sacred
mission. Naturally, the first visits were paid nearest
home, but the field of the propaganda was gradually extended until their absence embraced the period between
the rising and going down of the sun.

For a few days I was told all that occurred, exactly
what had been said on each vessel, how the tea tasted
with which they had been regaled, and even the spiteful remarks that the women on the other ships had made about
their neighbors. But, prompted by Donna Elenora, who
unconsciously was more of a logician than Fidette, the
leader of the Great Cause soon ceased to tell me anything. In this she was entirely within her own rights,
and I found no fault.

The Kantoon of the Cormorant, however, was not
so complacent, and on the first refusal of his wife to tell
him where she had been he reasserted the majesty of
man by locking her up in the sick bay and putting her
on a diet of dry seaweed and rainwater. He peremp-
torily refused to allow Donna Elenora to again accompany Fidette, and the splendid future of the good work
seemed to be imperiled. It was in vain that Fidette appealed to me to have her companion released. I told
her, candidly, that under the new order of things my influence did not extend to a control of the women in the
community; that, however much liberty I might allow

the gentle sex, I could not abolish the marriage relation or create any ex-post facto regulation that would abrogate the control that the husband was admitted to have over the conduct of the wife at the time the contract was made.

This didn't satisfy Fidette. Her estimate of man was no better than before. I was really charmed with the manner in which she stamped her little foot on the deck and said:

"Just wait till we control Sargasso and its myriad ships. We'll crucify such a man as Elenora's husband!"

This was perfectly delightful to me.

I learned from time to time that the social conditions on the ships that had been visited by the two priestesses of emancipation were quite the same as on board the Cormorant. The custom of giving teas to the visiting wives and daughters of the Kantoons had already practically destroyed one of the most sacred ordinances of the Sargassons forbidding the presence of fire on any ship. This offense, for which any man in the crew would have been instantly punished with death, was now committed by the ladies of Sargasso with impunity.

Another circumstances that I noticed in the line of independence was that they began bartering their jewels among each other, and the greater part of the personal property that had been the pride of the Sargasson people bid fair to drift into the hands of a few women who were shrewder and more skilled in the arts of barter than the others. I foresaw that this would lead to no end of trouble. Fidette was the superior of any woman in striking a bargain, and she did not, therefore, suffer especially at the hands of the shrewdest of her sex.

The catastrophe that I had feared came in a most startling and unexpected way.

Five months had been devoted to "ameliorating the condition of the Sargasson women." Her cares had been lightened to such an extent that she knew nothing about her own household as a rule, but was thoroughly acquainted with every detail regarding the affairs of her neighbors. She had begun to observe and comment upon the dress and the personal adornment of her best friends. She had taken to staining her cheeks with the juice of the ogalla berry—not to render her more beautiful and attractive to her husband, but to rouse the envy of her own sex.

Covetousness, a vice that had been unknown among these people previously, made its appearance, and some of the women devoted all their time to plotting how they might secure the most highly prized heirlooms that their friends possessed. Already several very scandalous charges have been made to the Chief Kantoon, involving undue influence and insinuating theft.

But the climax was reached one dark night, when the Sacred Light was flashed high into a sky of inky blackness. No intimation whatever as to the cause of its sudden appearance had been received over the searoot telegraph, and I have no doubt that on every ship, as on the Caribas, the deepest suspense was felt while the awful import of the glowing message in the sky was being slowly deciphered. With a movement, regular as the swinging of a pendulum, the searchlight was thrown east or west, north or south, southeast or northwest, until enough of the message had been imparted to enable every Sargasson to guess the rest.

I was not familiar enough in reading the signals of the Sacred Light to grasp the startling intelligence it conveyed. Fidette and my first officer, who stood near me, threw themselves upon their faces on the deck, exhibiting signs of abject terror. In vain I shook the first mate; then I strove to raise my wife to her feet.

Taking Fidette in my arms, I was about to carry her to her cabin, when I detected members of the crew dropping overboard from various parts of the ship. One sailor rushed past me, and threw himself headlong into

the sea. These acts of my men filled me with consternation. Before my eyes members of my crew were drowning themselves because of the information that the Sacred
Light had flashed to them!

Carrying Fidette to her cabin, I placed her on the
sofa, applied to her nostrils a bottle of strong salts that
had been in my locker, and she soon revived. I could
hear the men rushing about the deck in the utmost confusion. I was still completely mystified. My only hope
was an explanation from Fidette. The light in the cabin
was furnished by a large piece of rotten wood, suspended
from the ceiling by a cord. It was the fox-fire familiar
to all woodsmen. By the aid of this light I saw Fidette's eyes slowly open, but in them was a look of fear
and mental distress, such as I never saw exhibited by
a human being. I spoke to her again and again. I
entreated for an explanation. Suddenly she roused herself and sat bolt upright. She appeared oblivious of my
presence. She allowed me to take her hand, but appeared
unconscious of passionate and sympathetic words. Fi-
naly her lips moved, and she fairly screamed in a tone
of agony and remorse:

"We are lost!"

"Lost!" I exclaimed; "what has happened, my dar-
ling? What calamity can overcome us? I am here to
protect you. I can defend you against the entire power
of the Sargasson people—at least, I can do so as long
as there is life in me. Speak, sweet one. Do speak!"

"Oh, we are lost!" and the poor, little creature burst
into a hysterical fit of weeping. To no effect did I fold
her in my arms and hold her cheek close to mine, and,
somewhat rudely, perhaps, brushed the long, floating
hair from her cold brow. She would explain no further.

CHAPTER XXVII.

EVEN IN SARGASSO DOTH ENVY FIND A PLACE.

Leaving Fidette, I hurried upon deck, clutching the first mate, who, in a disordered condition of mind, was hurrying past me, and demanded to know from him the cause of the universal consternation. I detained him with difficulty, and it was several seconds before he was able to stammer out:

"The Sacred Flint has been stolen!"

"The sacred what?"

"The Sacred Flint, in the custody of the priest."

"Is that all?"

"Surely, that's enough," he gasped.

"What will come of it?" I asked, considerably relieved in mind.

"The Sacred Fire may burn out."

"I can understand that," was my answer, now feeling quite complacent.

"Our god will be in wrath. Not one of us will ever reach the Sweet Water Heaven."

"Too bad; anything else?" I inquired, now rather annoyed at all this ado about nothing.

"Yes; the thief, the one who has stolen this holy emblem—this sacred stone in which fire that water cannot quench is hidden—will be punished with a death so awful that the coldest Sargasson blood runs boiling hot at its contemplation. When found, he will be seized, taken to the ship of the Chief Kantoon, where his hands will be burned off, is eyes will be plucked out, and he will then be fastened to a spit and slowly roasted over the Sacred Fire that he has attempted to destroy. If, by a fatal mischance, the fire should be extinguished, he will then be cut into pieces while still alive and fed to the sacred sharks of the Inland Sea."

Having said this, the first mate saluted, and, with my permission, hurried away to rescue, if possible, by force, such members of the crew as had attempted suicide, but were unable to sink.

I returned to Fidette's side. She had ceased weeping. She was now more calm, but her face was ghastly pale. She now remembered me, and in the tenderest manner possible reached out her hands, taking mine that were extended toward her, and with quivering voice began:

"My dear husband, I am the cause of this dire calamity. I know how terrible must be my punishment; yet that is not what I fear, but the distress I have brought on others."

Then the suffering little woman had a nervous chill.

"Confide in me, Fidette," I began, sitting down close by her side to reassure her. "Tell me all."

"It happened in this way," Fidette began. "You know I gave a tea on board the Caribas two weeks ago, Saturday afternoon. Donna Elenora was here and assisted me, you will remember. Our tea was hot, contrary to the Sargasson custom. There never had been any fire on board the Cormorant, although on some of the other ships fires had been started surreptitiously by some of the wives of the Kantoons! The commander of the Cormorant had never permitted anything of the kind on board his ship.

"When, therefore, Donna Elenora, desiring to give a tea to-morrow, asked me for the loan of your flint, steel

and punk, in a thoughtless moment I declined to accede
to her request. I suggested that she borrow the flint
from the Priest of the Sacred Fire. She said nothing more,
but, going back to the gig that she was using, she at
once set out for the Inland Sea. I understand what
followed. She has gone to the ship of the Chief Kantoon
and has wheedled his daughter into lending the Sacred
Flint! My careless words inspired her. Envy counseled
her to commit this awful crime. She wanted to be like me.
She wanted to make a show. She has sacrificed her life,
that of her husband, and probably mine, to her vainglory
—not that I fear Death in his usual form, but, ugh! how I
shall hate to be roasted alive!"

"You shall not be punished, Fidette," I said, strok-
ing her pretty shoulders and speaking in my most affectionate tone. "I don't care what the law is; I don't care
a fig for the Sacred Flint. In the hold as ballast are
tons of flints. I will send the priest a boatload to-morrow. I shall appease his wrath. Comfort yourself, and
rest. You have distressed yourself too much. As for
Donna Elenora, let them roast her. Why should you
worry? She knew what she was about."

"My agony of mind is not wholly due to Elenora's
fate," admitted Fidette, hesitatingly. "You ask me to
lean upon you. You reassure me. You offer to extri-
cate me from my terrible situation and incidentally to
protect my life. I ought to refuse all your proffers.
Now that I am engaged in the rescue of women from the
a holy principle. This is a woman's crime, and by a
woman must it be atoned."

Fidette and I had lived happily together for almost
ten months. I never had been angry at her before. I
never had felt in all my life the impulse to strike or choke
dreadful domination of man, it is quite improper that I
should allow you to assert your authority over others,
even in my behalf. No; I must die. I must suffer for
a woman, but at this moment out of the depths of my

soul arose a demoniacal impulse to snatch Fidette from the couch on which she lay, hurl her to the floor and jump on her. Her talk was such utter nonsense, so repugnant to the better part of a man's nature, such an exhibition of heartless ingratitude, that no mere man could endure it. Of course, I mastered the influence. I did nothing. I simply walked out upon deck and beat my head against the mainmast.

Meanwhile the commotion on the ship had increased rather than diminished. All discipline had been cast to the winds. In the darkest shadows of the deck I could see the men standing together in groups conversing in their horrible polyglotic language. I felt that some action ought to be taken looking to the assertion of my authority.

In the loudest voice I could command. I called away every boat that the ship possessed. Then, taking five men with me, I descended into the hold, knowing the way perfectly in the murky darkness, and there commanded each member of my crew to carry as much of the stone ballast to the deck as he could lift. The flint had been broken into all sizes, but I had trouble to prevent the men from undertaking to carry too much. One would have supposed that they would have selected the smaller pieces, but, on the contrary, they selected the largest they could find.

When we reached the deck, I called the ship's company around me, told them I had learned of the terrible disaster that had overtaken the Priest of the Holy Fire, and concluded by stating that each of the pieces of stone then heaped upon the deck contained enough hidden fire to keep the flames of the Sargasson priesthood aglow all eternity. They received my statement with incredulity at first, but when I seized a hammer and struck from a score or more of the jagged stones the glinting sparks that evidenced the presence of hidden fire the men burst into a shout of joy. They manned the twenty boats, in the centre of each was placed at least a bushel of the precious flints, and, without waiting for further orders, they set off in the darkness up the Grand Canal toward the Inland Sea to deliver their priceless cargo to the Priest of the Sacred Fire.

I then commanded the executive officer to put in operation the sea-root telegraph, in order that the suspense under which the Chief Kantoon and his priesthood were suffering might be at once relieved. I know that fully two hours would be required to transmit the message from ship to ship, and had some anxiety regarding its form and character when it should have reached its destination after passing through so many hands, but at the end of two hours I had the satisfaction of seeing the Sacred Fire again flashing in the skies, and, aided by the first mate as interpreter, I learned that the Chief Kantoon reassured his people that the Sacred Fire would never go out.

Having roused Fidette from her troubled sleep I joyfully told her that danger and misfortune were past. In a few brief sentences I explained to her the sending of the twenty boats loaded with flints.

Never did mortal give such a deep sigh of relief as did Fidette, and, throwing her arms about my neck, she said:

"How much easier and better it is to have somebody to do my thinking for me. I have been a silly woman."

CHAPTER XXVIII.

PLOTTING TREASON.

My escape from Sargasso was due largely to Fidette. Through her I secured the command of my vessel, the Caribas.

Do you wonder that I loved her?

The fidelity of Fidette to me extended to acts of treason to her native community. Although the great world was to her only a tradition she had developed a deep longing to live, as her mother had done, upon land, and to escape forever from the uneasy, unquiet sea.

One of my first acts on assuming control of the Caribas was to remove the men's quarters from the centre of the ship. The first mate was provided with apartments directly underneath my own, and he was glad of the change. My purpose in making these transfers was to render it possible for me to thoroughly overhaul the engines of the Caribas in the hope that they could be restored to effectiveness. The various small and vital parts of the engine that had been taken away had been distributed among the other ships nearby, where they were regarded as souvenirs. These, by her admirable art of making and cultivating friendships on the other vessels, Fidette was able to secure, and one by one return to the ship. This labor of appreciation and love occupied much time.

Thanks to my knowledge of marine engineering I was able to readjust the various parts, and when they were all in place I gave the engine the finishing touches one night during a violent storm of thunder and lightning, when the necessary hammering could not be heard by the crew. I next secured great quantities of seaweed, to be used under the boilers, especially the waxy and oleaginous kinds that come from the mouth of the Amazon. When thoroughly dried I was confident these plants would burn admirably. Wood was also procured from the floating logs.

On one of the large mahogany trees, covered with parasitic plants and vines, we encountered a huge anaconda. It had evidently been brought down the Amazon in one of the Spring freshets, and had sustained itself, probably for many months, upon the birds, nautili, crayfish and anaimalculae that gathered upon the branches of the floating trunk.

My audacious plan was to take the Caribas to sea and to trust to encountering a tow. She was the latest and most valuable possession of the Sargassons. She was valued for her enduring qualities far above any other ship they possessed.

I finally reached a stage in which it was absolutely necessary to take somebody, at least partially, into my confidence. I had carefully studied the members of the crew, and had fixed upon a man for my purpose. He was the boatswain, and I knew by my own experience as a deep-water sailor that that subordinate officer is rarely popular with the crew. I therefore hoped that, by attaching him to my interests and encouraging him to hope for advancement, I could make sure of his secrecy. I sent for him one night and broached the subject.

We stood alone on the quarter deck to make sure that nobody was within hearing distance. I led him to believe that what I contemplated was securing a better berth for the Caribas. Without being guilty of abso-

lute falsehood, I caused him to think that I had permission to move the vessel out of the narrow strait in which
we were berthed to the large lagoon just out of the
Grand Canal and in close proximity to the Inland Sea.

This was the highly aristocratic part of Sargasso, and
the boatswain was delighted.

After the watch had been set and the ship's company had gone to sleep I visited the engine room, the
key of which I carefully guarded, and found the machinery
in excellent condition. I saw the necessity of being provided with plenty of oil for the engine, and directed that
fifty porpoises should be harpooned and their fat tried
out. This oil I stored in some empty water casks.

How could I prevent the smoke from being observed? Fires would have to be lighted under the boilers fully a day to generate sufficient steam to move the
engines. The moment a huge volume of smoke was
seen to issue from the funnels of the Caribas a general
signal would be flashed from the ship of the Chief Kantoon, and before we could hope to get under way we
would be beset on all sides by at least one thousand
canoes, each manned by two blood-thirsty Sargasson
devils, who, despite our efforts at defense (and I could
not count upon my crew), would swarm aboard the ship
and literally carve us to pieces.

The Sargassons acted strictly upon the motto, "Dead
men tell no tales." They did not intend that anybody
should ever escape from Sargasso, and I have always believed that the sad end of Arthur Gray was due to the
fact that the Chief Kantoon had, under Gray's artful per-
suasions, allowed him the privilege, never accorded to
any other Sargasson, of revisiting his native land. Popular as he was said to have been prior to that time, it was
notorious that he was regarded with suspicion after his
return. Of course, I knew of no reason for such distrust.
Gray had added one of the finest vessels to the community, and that ought to have evoked gratitude.

But gratitude is as rare in Sargasso as in the more highly civilized parts of the world.

The problem of preventing the smoke from becoming visible was solved by Fidette. Since her active labors for the regeneration of woman among the Sargassons it had become a very common custom for the daughters and wives of the Kantoons to do cooking surreptitiously on board their ships. Many of them could now broil a bloater or make a crayfish chowder equal to the best Fulton Market cook. In order to do this they had had to devise means by which the presence of fire and smoke was disguised. They had found that crushed barnacles, mixed with bits of salt-encrusted wood sprinkled upon the fire, destroyed the carbon in the smoke and caused it to assume a yellowish hue. It then readily assimilated with the dense atmosphere of the mid-Atlantic, and was not observable during the night by the men on watch on the other ships. During daylight I feared that the keen-eyed Sargassons would detect the presence of heat by the currents in the atmosphere; but some risks had to be taken.

Under the pretext of providing better comforts for the men and giving them more privacy, I had the fore part of the deck cut up into cabins, with accommodations for eight sailors in each. My purpose was to separate the men into groups so that I could handle them. I dared not trust the entire ship's company at liberty. I had calculated that eight stokers would be sufficient to keep the fires going. In one of the lockers that had remained untouched I had a gross of padlocks, and these I intended to utilize upon the doors of the rooms. The plan was to march the eight men to the boiler room under the charge of the boatswain and myself. We would then lock them in, with the understanding that they were to have eight hours of continuous work, after which they would be relieved

The boatswain was to stand guard over them at the

head of the iron ladder, where he readily could defend himself, because of the inaccessibilty of the position. I carefully instructed Fidette about the machinery, as I expected to have to rely upon her to answer the calls of the bell in the engine room.

I hoped to get the vessel well under way and then to remain in the wheelhouse myself long enough to effect our escape. Once out upon the broad Atlantic, it did not matter very much whether the engine broke down or the fuel gave out. If we could gain one hundred miles of offing we would be in the track of vessels bound for the Canary Islands, and might hope to be picked up before long.

The greatest problem was the feeding of the crew during the semi-imprisonment. This serious question was solved by my recollecting that fifty barrels of salt pork and one hundred barrels of hard crackers, hermetically sealed, had been stowed in the hold; and an examination showed that these provisions had escaped discovery during the possession of the ship by the Sargassons. This greatly encouraged me. Apparently, Providence had special interest in my behalf.

Another detail that I had planned was to send the first mate on a fictitious mission to the Gassoon, a neighboring derelict. Several of the most untrustworthy members of the crew could also be dispatched on the weekly voyage for provisions, just prior to my departure.

I knew very well, as I have already stated, that the agitation for universal rights among the ships had utterly destroyed the rigidness of the discipline that had formerly existed, and I hoped to be able to allay the curiosity of my crew when they discovered that fires were burning under the boilers by telling them that I was about to prepare a great feast for their entertainment.

Every day's delay added to my danger.

At roll call one morning a member of our ship's company was missing. A search of the most rigid character, in which I joined, because of my anxiety, failed to find him anywhere on board. I had the boats counted, and none was missing. If he were a fugitive the man had escaped over the floating sod—a very difficult act in the darkness. The chances of his reaching any other vessel by that means were infinitesimally small. Not to mention the dangers encountered from the poisonous snakes and scorpions that infested the vines and parasite growths upon the tree tops, the fugitive could not avoid thin places in the sod that would appear safe to the eye, but would yield at once to the slightest pressure of the foot.

The mystery of this sailor's absence was never explained, but from the hour of his disappearance until I was safely out of the Seaweed Sea I did not pass a moment without anxiety.

CHAPTER XXIX.

THE CARIBAS UNDER STEAM.

To the final council with the boatswain Fidette was admitted. That afternoon I had turned the engine over by hand, and knew that every piece of its mechanism was in place. I realized the danger of further delay, and decided that the break for liberty should be made on the following night.

In the mean time it was necessary to obtain possession of all the arms carried by the ship's company, although a demand to that effect would certainly arouse suspicion. All the cutlasses that had been placed about the ship for emergencies were quietly gathered up and put under lock in the main cabin. We had no firearms. The only other weapons to be feared were the large knives carried by the members of the crew, which, unfortunately, they knew only too well how to use. We deliberated for an hour or more as to the means of obtaining these, when Fidette offered a suggestion that made it very easy.

"Among the crew," she began, "is a little old man who was once a scissors grinder. He often sings to himself about the days when he tramped the streets and roads of his native land, bell in hand, in search of knives and scissors to grind. There are several grindstones in the hold. Now, I propose to rig up one of these for him

on the main deck, and send word to all members of the
crew that they can have their knives ground. Each sailor
can be told to put a mark upon his knife so that it can be
returned to him. In this way we shall get all these weapons into our possession.

The idea was so feasible that I adopted it at once.

I confess that I was very anxious about our voyage
on the Grand Canal, en route to the open sea. The
Caribas would have to pass in plain sight of several hundred Sargasson derelicts. You may say that I knew that
the vessels were without armament, that solid shot
would not be fired across our bow, and that we
ought to have known that we could keep off boarders
when well under headway? And yet I was tempted to
give up the venture, and to end my days among the Sargassons.

Deep down in my heart I felt shame and mortification at the thought of what my brother Kantoons in Sargasso would think and say of me. Among them the
taking away of my own ship would undoubtedly be regarded as theft! My treachery would be looked upon
as of the most infamous kind. My name would be posted
on the blacklist in the cabin of the Chief Kantoon, and
forever held up to universal execration.

With my infamy, poor Fidette's name would be
linked. She was a Sargasson by birth, and to her the
forswearing of her people meant much, in sentiment and
in fact. She was of the Water Worshipers, and nowhere
else on the face of the earth would she find people of her
faith! She was deeply religious, and her willingness to
follow me into an unknown part of the world, where people dwelt upon solid land (incomprehensible as that appeared to her) was an undeniable proof of her affection.

I was deeply affected by all these thoughts. It was
only a few months since the Sargassons had loaded me
with honors. The ceremonial by which I had been cre-
ated Kantoon of the Caribas was one of the most im-

posing and splendid that had ever been known in Sargasso. These facts only emphasized my ingratitude.

I cannot expect any of my readers to understand the feelings that welled up in my heart, because they have not dwelt among the Sargasson people, and cannot appreciate the high and peculiar sense of honor that there obtains.

In addition to all these pretty sentiments, I was afraid to give up the scheme, having once undertaken it. I feared the treachery of the boatswain! His first overindulgence in rainwater might loosen his tongue and he might divulge my secret. My punishment would be swift. The most merciful end I could expect would be death by drowning; but I have since learned from Fidette that the only treacherous Kantoon she recalls was strapped upon a heavy water butt, which was then rolled about the deck until the body of the condemned was crushed into pulp.

It was too late for me to retreat; I must escape or die in an ignominious manner.

On the morning following our final conference the boatswain found a small grindstone, already mounted, brought it to the deck and set the grinder to work. The old man was delighted. He trod the pedal with all the glee of youth, and as the sparks flew he laughed and sang.

THE KNIFE-GRINDER'S SONG.

The dogfish needs no grinder stout,
His teeth are in his head;
The whale he takes his molars out,
And puts 'em 'side his bed.
But the swordfish, he
Engages me—
His dentist, don't you see.
"Too-ra-loo-ra-loo-ra-loo"—
The wheel sings when I sing.
"Too-ra-loo-ra-loo ra loo;
Too-ra-loo-ra-bur-r-r-r!"

The air was a quaint one, and recalled the first six bars in "The Boatswain's Story," by Malloy. The

words, however, were Sargasson, and the above translation is very liberal.

The men hardly had to be asked to surrender their
knives. They gave them up voluntarily, so anxious
were they to have their blades bright and sharp. The
weapons were placed in a box that I had prepared for
them. In order to delay matters I gave the grinder half
a dozen cutlasses from my own cabin that were to be finished before the knives were ground. All day long, almost without a moment's rest, the old knife-grinder
tramped and sang as the rusty steel struck prickly stars
from the whirring wheel.

That night the men occupied their new apartments
for the first time. They were delighted at the comforts
I had prepared for them. They readily divided themselves up into watches and associated themselves together
in groups of eight. New bedding had been prepared for
all the men. The bunks were filled with the driest and
softest sea grass obtainable, thus forming a bed as soft
as a hair mattress. I wanted them to sleep well this first
night. I had so divided the men that the first watch
was composed of thoroughly tractable members of the
crew.

The moment night fell the boatswain and I repaired
to the boiler room. He soon struck a light with flint
and steel, and in a few moments we had the fires aglow.
Leaving him in charge for the moment, after seeing that
he was thoroughly armed, I returned to the deck and
saw that all the ship's company had retired to their new
and sumptuous sleeping apartments.

The ideal existence of the Sargasson sailor is to have
plenty of time to sleep and all the food he wants to eat.
As I had supposed, everybody had gone to bed except
the eight men on watch. I quietly closed the doors of all
the compartments and secured them with the heavy padlocks.

I then mustered the watch, and marched them direct-

ly to the furnace room. There I found the boatswain
working like a demon to keep the furnaces full of wood
and seaweed. The sailors regarded the open mouth of
the flaming furnaces with reverential awe. How natural
is man's worship of the elements. As it happened, they
were all Sargassons born and bred. They could not possibly understand the purpose for which the fire was burning, but at my command they fell lustily to work under
the direction of the boatswain. Carefully fastening the
heavy iron door behind me, I ascended to the engine
room to watch the steam gauge.

Hours must elapse before I could hope to move the
engine, and in the mean time I sought out Fidette, who
was sitting at her cabin window, gazing thoughtfully out
upon the night.

Only then had she begun to realize the seriousness
of the change about to come over her life. She knew
also that we had gone so far that in the event of failure,
exposure and punishment would be certain. I tried to
reassure her. I told her that, if under a sufficient head
of steam, the engine did not work, not a man, including
the boatswain, would be allowed to escape from the furnace room. I would descend and slaughter every one
of them with my own hand rather than expose myself,
and especially her, to the punishment that certainly would
await us. This was a dreadful thing to say, but I had
calmly resolved upon the extinction of these nine members of the crew in case of failure. No questions were
ever asked in Sargasso regarding the disappearance of
men on ship board, and I could not be expected to account for the missing members of the crew.

As I should have explained, I had filled the boilers
with sea water by opening the valves connected with the
pumps outside the ship. Careful measurement had
shown me that the boilers were all below the water line.
After steam was once generated, I knew that the pumps
could be utilized to keep the boilers filled.

You can imagine, therefore, with what anxiety I stood in the engine room and watched the slow but sure rising of the steam gauge. I believed a pressure of eighty pounds to the square inch would be required to get under way. The engines were of the most modern triple expansion type. I did not aim at high speed, for I believed that attack would be impossible if I could obtain a headway of ten or twelve miles an hour.

Fidette soon joined me in the engine room. The register now showed twenty-one pounds! I softly rang the bell connecting with the boatswain, and called down through the tube, telling him to redouble the efforts of the men, and acquainting him with the fact that steam was already forming. He replied at once that the men were stuffing the furnaces with wood and pulpy seaweed. But the influence of my words upon him produced immediate results, as shown by the steam gauge. It began' slowly to turn upon the disk.

Forty pounds were soon indicated! In another quarter of an hour the pressure had risen to forty-seven! Soon it was fifty, and I felt that in another hour I would be able to make the supreme test.

What would be the result? Would the piston, after having remained for two years stationary in the cylinder, move when the steam pressure was admitted? My life itself depended upon the answer to that question—if not the lives of Fidette and myself, certainly those of the nine men in the bowels of the ship!

CHAPTER XXX.

FAREWELL TO THE FLOATING CONTINENT.

Having sent Fidette back to her cabin—for I did not wish her to witness my mortification in the event of failure—I approached the steam gauge and looked it fairly in the face.

Seventy-five pounds of steam pressure were indicated.

The moment had come!

I stepped promptly to the rack in which had rested during all these months the long, slender steel lever with which the engine had always been started. I took it down and fitted it in place. Then, having signaled to the boatswain that I was about to make the trial, I quickly opened the valve, and, having allowed a few moments to pass in order that the hot steam might impart some of its warmth to the large pipes and to the cylinder, I swung the lever, as I had often done before on the Caribas and other steamers.

To my horror, the cylinder did not respond. Again and again I shut off the steam and suddenly admitted it, in the hope that the shock might start the rusty piston in the cylinder.

Then I bethought me of a venturesome experiment. Hastily allowing the steam to escape from the upper end of the cylinder, I unscrewed one of the oil cups, and, having procured a pint of sulphuric acid from the locker in which the chemicals were kept, I diluted it three times with water, and poured the mixture into the top of the cylinder. It was a very risky thing to do; but I remembered that diluted sulphuric acid was used for removing verdigris (which is the corrosion on brass, just as rust is the oxidation on iron), and it had seemed to me the most natural way of cleansing the interior of the cylinder. I hastily replaced the oil cup, using the first wrench I could find for the purpose.

I waited ten minutes for the sulphuric acid to accomplish its work. Then I gave the wheel that opened connection with the boilers a savage twist, throwing the valve wide open and suddenly admitting to the cylinder the full head of steam, now registering eighty-five pounds of pressure.

At the first stroke of the lever I knew that the engine was going to work. In twenty seconds more it was running on its own momentum. Its mechanism was somewhat halting and unsteady, but I could feel that the shaft communicating with the propeller was revolving.

I hurried on deck and, with an axe already provided, I cut away the heavy strands of seaweed cable that held us to the adjacent tree trunks. With a few blows of a sledge hammer I knocked the heavy anchor chain out of the bitts, where it had been held for two years, and it escaped overboard through the hawse hole, serpentlike, attended with a noise like thunder.

In a minute more we were steaming along the Grand Canal!

Fidette had been recalled to the engine room, and I was now in the wheelhouse. To my delight I found that the Caribas answered the helm perfectly. As soon as we had emerged from the dock-like berth in which the vessel had been moored into the broad expanse of the Grand Canal I slowly swung the bow of the Caribas to the westward, and headed her out to sea.

We passed so close to the Happy Shark that I could have thrown a biscuit on board. But all was silence thereon. Nowhere in the semi-darkness could I descry a moving object. We were then passing the scene of the attack by the pirates of the Spar, and I recalled all the incidents of that desperate contest. Despite the thrilling sensations of freedom, my ears still rang with the cries of the dying and the shouts of the victors.

Fortunately for me, in my early apprenticeship on the sea, I had served many watches at the wheel. During my stay in Sargasso, with the hope of escape ever present before me, I had taken careful bearings of the Grand Canal as the only recognized watery path to the ocean, and, although it had not a beacon or other commanding headland, I had no fear of misadventure.

Through the tube communicating with the engine room I encouraged Fidette, and by similar means implored the boatswain to stand by the torrid furnaces.

To my unbounded delight and surprise the Caribas was now doing as well as she had ever done under my command. The gummy, resinous character of the seaweed was developing more boiler power than had ever been extracted from coal. I learned from Fidette that the steam gauge showed a pressure of 115 pounds.

We were speeding away from this detested community at the rate of fifteen miles an hour!

The darkness was so intense that I felt confident we had not even been missed. If our movements had been heard by any of the ships along the canal I knew that an interval of at least an hour would be required to communicate the fact to the Chief Kantoon. But the curious system of marine telegraphy, which I have described, was complete and effective; and when my treason was detected the Priest of the Sacred Fire would be notified.

We were nearing the outer barrier of seaweed when I detected from the wheelhouse (which, following the fashion of the American coastwise steamers, had been placed in the forward part of the ship) a dark object moving over the face of the black waters. I knew instinctively that it was a barge filled with Sargassons, and the demoniacal impulse filled my heart to have one last bit of revenge for the barbarous and inhuman manner in which they had massacred my crew.

I changed the course of the Caribas two points and headed directly for the great canoe. Like an avenging genii out of the darkness I bore down upon it. The men at the paddles were utterly paralyzed with fear. They could not understand the presence of this huge craft, and by their inaction were an easy mark for the blow I dealt them amidships. The barge was crushed like an egg-shell, and the thirty men were thrown into the water. Those that escaped being drawn under the Caribas by the suction or ground to pieces by the propeller were devoured by sharks or run through by swordfish.

The open water of the ocean lay directly ahead!

In another quarter of an hour we had passed the place at which the Caribas had fallen a prey to Sargasson treachery. Assured that we were clear of all entangling grass I made the wheel fast and hurried to the engine room, where I kissed and embraced Fidette—first announcing through the tube to the faithful boatswain that we had escaped. I examined the water cocks, started the pumping engine and replenished the depleted boilers. Then I went carefully over the engine and oiled every part(after which, taking Fidette by the hand, I led her on deck, en route to the pilot house.

As we ascended the main companionway into the blackness of the night Fidette stopped short in her walk and exclaimed:

"Behold! See the Sacred Fire! Our flight is known throughout the Seaweed Sea!"

There, high in the sky, stood the vivid pillar of fire, waving to and fro!

Fidette interpreted the signals that announced my infamous treachery. The proclamation took this form:

"The Caribas is gone! Her Kantoon shall die. A Kantoonship to his captor!"

I took Fidetté, dear little creature, in my arms, and, as I kissed her, said:

"They are too late, my pet. Our next address, I hope, will be New York."

*   *   *   *   *   *   *   *   *   *

It is quite needless to prolong this narrative further. After two days' steaming due north the fuel was exhausted and our engine ceased to work. I constructed, from all the blankets on board ship, staysails, with which I was able to keep the Caribas out of the trough of the sea. I gave liberty to only eight members of the crew at a time.

For four days we rode out the ocean swell. We were sighted by the German steamer Nordland, bound from Gibraltar to New York. She soon came within hailing distance. The Nordland's second officer was sent aboard us. To him I recounted briefly our situation. He returned to his ship, and twenty men came to aid me in bringing the Caribas into port.

A line was passed to us, and six days of slow steaming brought us to New York, where we anchored in the Horseshoe.

All the cities of America are great; but New York —New York is greatest of all, because it owes everything to the sea.

Fidette came ashore with me, and her emotions when she first beheld houses and city streets were curious.

The arrival of the Caribas was cabled to Europe, of course, and late the next afternoon our agents on this side of the water received the following telegram:

"Austin Clark, New York:

  "Proceed Santos, then Buenos Ayres for orders.

        "TRIPPLETT & JONES."

Utterly without sentiment, curiosity, or—gratitude, are some shipowners.

THE END.

www.ingramcontent.com/pod-product-compliance
Lightning Source LLC
Chambersburg PA
CBHW022356020726
47500CB00002B/306